The Tangled Web

Edited by Lauren Lyn Cidell

Published by Purple Crystal, an imprint of Purple Turkey
Press
www.purpleturkeypress.com

Copyright © 2018 Lauren Lyn Cidell
Published by Lauren Lyn Cidell / Purple Turkey
Press
ISBN 978-0-9997515-8-9

Cover art by Toni Johnson

This book would not have happened without the generous moral and financial support of my family, my friends Donna and Shawn, and especially my fellow Inklings: Chris Gerrib, Don Hunt, Toni Johnson, Wren Roberts, and Pete Borger

Pete, this one's for you.

ACKNOWLEDGMENTS

Introduction copyright © 2018 by Lauren Lyn Cidell

"The Gathering at Spider Hill" copyright © 2013 by Donald J. Hunt

"Weaver Of Dreams" Excerpt from DREAMS MADE FLESH by Anne Bishop, copyright © 2005 by Anne Bishop. Used by permission of New American Library, an imprint of Penguin Publishing Group, a division of Penguin Random House LLC. All rights reserved.

"The Spider Under The Bed" copyright © 2017 by Chris Gerrib

"Spinster" copyright © 2016 by Lauren Lyn Cidell

Excerpt from AGE OF ANANSI, copyright © 2012 by James Lovegrove, Used with permission of James Lovegrove

"Separate from the Animals" copyright © 2018 by Jason Evans

"The Courtship Dance" copyright © 2018 by Jennifer Lee Rossman

"Webinar: Web Sites" copyright © 2018 by Steven H Silver

"Sons of the Spider" copyright © 2016 by Toni Johnson

"Anansi and Brother Death…or Why Spider's Webs Are Found On The Ceiling" copyright © 2007 by Michael Auld, Used with permission of Michael Auld

"The Entomologist's Discovery" copyright © 2017 by Wren Roberts

"Taste Test" copyright © 2016 by Joshua Byrd

"Vengeance" copyright © 2017 by Pete Borger.

Afterword copyright © 2018 by Lauren Lyn Cidell

CONTENTS

Introduction

By Lauren Lyn Cidell

From Anansi of Africa to the Grandmother Spiders of the Americas, arachnids have a firm niche in the human cultural psyche. They have been creators and tricksters, sometimes helping humanity, sometimes harming.

Spiders are the subject of numerous superstitions all over the world portending events good, bad, and neutral. They are mentioned in both the Bible and the Qu'ran. Arachnophobia was the first phobia documented, as well being one as the most common. I myself am something of an arachnophobe. This begs the question: why would I assemble an anthology themed around a creature I fear?

Well, in 2013, Don Hunt submitted a first draft of "The Gathering at Spider Hill" to our writers' group for a critique. It gave me nightmares. Two years later when Toni Johnson submitted "Sons of the Spider" (which also gave me nightmares) the idea of an arachnid anthology was first suggested by Pete.

Pete was a prolific writer. His style reminded me of Rod Serling: nothing was ever what it seemed, especially his female characters. I half expected him to write a story featuring a *jorōgumo,* a Japanese demon in the guise of a beautiful woman who seduces men with her music and then uses spider silk to hold them captive and eat them.

Pete's passing was a stark reminder of suddenly a life can end and how every moment should be well spent. At our first meeting after his memorial, we decided to go through with the anthology and dedicate it to him.

The Gathering at Spider Hill

by Donald J. Hunt

Donald J. Hunt grew up near Rochester, New York, where his love of writing was kindled, no pun intended, through impromptu writing contests in Mrs. Shannon's fifth grade class. Those early explorations into the imagination sparked a nagging passion to weave tales. That insistence ebbed and flowed but never left. *Jupiter Justice* is his first complete novel.

His life journey eventually took him to the suburbs of Chicago, Illinois. He lives there now with his wife and two children. He is striving to indoctrinate the children into the ways of the Force and all things Geek. The dog, Cooper, and the cat, Buffy the Vampire Slayer, wholeheartedly support his endeavors.

As Ray Canfield turned into the subdivision, he bit his lower lip. Worry for his niece, Amanda, ate at him, and he took a deep breath to keep himself calm. He hated driving through the Sunnyside development, but Amanda lived here, and he needed to check on her. Her latest texts had been unsettling.

Unfortunately, the Acres boy also lived in here. Ever since the spider incident, he shuddered every time he saw the kid. Ray hated spiders. His older brother used to pin him down and put spiders on his face, letting them crawl around while Ray screamed until he was hoarse. In third grade, his brother had put a fist-sized wolf spider in Ray's lunch box. It had freaked him out so much when he'd gone to get his peanut butter and jelly sandwich that he leaped backward, tripped, and knocked himself out on the bench seat behind him. Although the years of tormenting by spider had stopped after that, the terror had remained. As the new Fire Chief, this posed some embarrassing challenges, but he got by.

Ray drove slowly into the 'new' subdivision on the west side of town. The tires of his red 2008 Explorer scrunched over some loose gravel that had blown onto the tar road. A faded sign with a couple of bullet holes in it read, "Welcome to Sunnyside! Custom Homes in the low 500s! Visit our Model Home today!" Someone had spray-painted "Up" next to Sunnyside in large yolk-orange letters. Just beyond that, the model home stood vacant, a board over the front window from the time some kids had thrown rocks through it. Brand new roads and curbs had been put in place, pipes and electrical wiring laid, but other than the model home in the front, and six houses in the way back, empty lots full of weeds, barren dirt and scattered stones dominated the scene. Ray shook his head in sadness. Woulda been good for the town, for sure. His hometown of Braeburn, Illinois needed a break. Lots of folks had lost jobs and hadn't been able to find new ones with the economy all bollixed up.

He saw the model home in his rearview and shook his head again, this time in annoyance. That house would probably need to be torn down. The idiots in Electrical always shut the damn electric off without getting the water turned off first. Sure enough, pipes burst come winter. Water had been running down the outside of the house for days, if not weeks, from the second floor until he'd noticed it and shut the water off himself. It'll take a miracle to get all the black mold out of that place now. Save a few pennies and ruin the tax base. Sure, brilliant.

A split in the road veered off to the right. Ray took it and wound his way up the hill and into the semi-wooded area in the back. As he drove past the first three empty houses, each in various stages of completion, he saw that all looked quiet tonight. The fourth house was a charred ruin of blackened beams sticking up like the lower mandible of some great, ebon-toothed leviathan from a bygone age. Teens had burned the place, intentionally or not, last spring, shortly before the last two houses were bought for a third of what they were worth. If you didn't mind driving through a wasteland, then you could get quite a deal.

The burned out husk was one reason why he had taken to patrolling the subdivision. The other reason was Amanda Harding. She lived in the fifth house up the hill, and she also happened to be his cousin Shelly's kid from a first marriage and called him Uncle Ray. Ray loved his cousin and Amanda, but didn't have much use for her second husband, Tim. Tim's only redeeming quality had been that he'd moved the family back to Braeburn two years ago.

However, moving into a small town can be tough when all the clichés and social dynamics have already been in play for over a decade. Amanda didn't quite fit in. Every day, after school, Amanda walked over to the fire station, and they visited while he drove Amanda home. They talked about books, movies, teachers, and favorite foods. Amanda's was chocolate ice cream, which Ray argued was not a food, while the young lady doggedly insisted it was, with an impish smile above her pointed chin. Straight, lifeless, dusty-brown hair hung down to a small nose when it fell forward, and a few barely noticeable freckles adorned her cheeks.

Last week, he'd seen Tim at the house. He looked terrible. Thin, sallow-skinned and with a distracted expression on his face. Damp or greasy hair hung down his forehead, and a sheen of perspiration clung to his face, as if he'd been working out, but he wore jeans and a button shirt. When Tim had opened the door and seen Ray, he started backward.

"Jesus. I thought you were that pest, Johansson. Why do firefighters need a uniform anyway?"

"Ed? The police chief? Why? What's he want with you?"

"Nothing." Tim curled his lip in distaste. "Never mind. I've got to get back to work."

"What's his deal?" Ray had asked Amanda, regretting the question immediately. Amanda's less than enthusiastic relationship to her stepfather was no secret between them, but Ray tried to keep a sympathetic yet neutral stance.

Amanda grabbed two soda cans from the fridge and shrugged. They sat on barstools at an island, which also housed the dishwasher and sink and faced the fridge. Thin wisps of cobwebs interwove the sconces of the light over the island--a four pronged thing that looked more like an anchor than a lamp. More fine webs wafted in the corners. The kitchen opened up to the family room on the north side, and he could see more cobwebs around the TV and a floor lamp. Mentally, he shook his head.

Popping open the soda, she said, "He's been even more skeevy since the Acres moved in. He's been hanging around with Tod Acres and his parents a lot. Tod told me that he spells his name wrong on purpose to annoy teachers. Like they would care. Dickhead."

Ray ignored that. "Hanging out doing what?"

She shrugged again. "Research. Experiments. Dunno. Really whack stuff. Something about spiders. Come on, I'll show you."

Ray felt his stomach go cold and then hot. A tremor of nausea rippled through him. He took a swig of the soda.

"No, thanks. I don't want to interrupt your dad."

"He's in the basement. I mean his books. C'mon you big baby." She gave him a teasing grin and hopped off the barstool with all the joy of a kid embarking on a forbidden escapade and hurried across the living room. Along the north wall, beyond the family room, were a laundry room, a small bathroom and, in the northeast corner, furthest from the street, Tim's office.

"Look. He's been reading all these like crazy." She pointed at a three-foot particleboard bookcase along the wall. Four entire shelves were jammed with books piled on top of other books. Ray set his soda on top, next to a fish tank, and squatted down to scan the titles. All on spiders, scientific and fantastic. *Spider Temples of Ancient Peru, Handbook of Neurotoxicology, Spider Venoms and Antivenins, The Wisdom of Anansi the Spider God, The Cult of Uttu.*

He reached up and grabbed his soda. As he did so, he caught movement out of the corner of his eye. He realized with a sinking feeling that the glass habitat at eye level was not a fish tank, but instead a terrarium. Blue stones, a couple of shells, and the greenery had misled him at first. From under the plastic plants, a furry shape charged out from beneath a fake rock and thumped into the glass inches from his face. Amanda squeaked, which did not help his reaction. His jerked backward, and soda flew out of the can high in the air.

He looked at Amanda, with soda in her hair and dripping down her face, and they both started laughing. She ran to get a towel, and he took a closer look at his stalker. A tarantula or something like it. The face and legs were aqua-toothpaste-blue, with large hairy fangs hanging down in front, like frickin' walrus tusks, and the body was striped orange, reminiscent of a tiger. He grimaced at the sight, and the spider lunged at him again, slamming into the glass over and over.

"Sonuvabitch," he mumbled to himself. "I've never heard of an aggressive pet tarantula." He stood up and a shiver started in his shoulders and ran along his spine.

He turned, about to call out to Amanda, wondering where she had gotten to, and there stood Tim, his hands gripping Amanda by the shoulder, a falcon clutching its prey. Beside him stood Tod Acres. Grinning. As angry as Tim was, his eyes bulging, mouth in a tight line, Ray could only look at Tod.

The boy smiled, his hands in his pockets like a miniature store manager. The kid, maybe twelve, had a blond flattop haircut, with the rounded cheeks and belly that reminded Ray of some cartoon character; he had the look of a kid who sat around playing too many computer games, eating too many donuts, and would get off on setting houses on fire. Ray had seen him downtown one day, when he was stuck at a traffic light. The kid was standing on the corner, a foot from Ray's truck. He had stuck his tongue out at him, like kids do when they're sucking on a candy, and they want to show it off. He'd

16

had a dark oval on his tongue. Ray didn't think much of it. He'd even smiled at the kid. He looked at the traffic light and back and the kid was pulling the piece of candy out. Only it wasn't candy.

The thing unfolded, wriggling in the boy's fingers; the kid switched it to the palm of his other hand. It was a spider. A small wolf spider, a little bigger than a quarter. Ray had jumped, spilled his coffee in his lap, and sworn at the wet heat and the unexpected sight. Sometime around then, the light had turned green and the guy behind him started honking his horn. He'd driven off and the kid had watched him go, grinning. Just like he was now.

Tim's anger finally sputtered into truncated half-speech. "What. Are. You doing in. My. Office?"

"Um, looking for a book?" Ray gave an apologetic grin. He felt foolish with soda on his face. "Sorry about the mess. Spider scared me."

"Get. Out."

Later that Friday night, he got a text from Amanda:

SD pissed. Gotta take bus for awhile. Sorry. :(

He had not seen her at all this past week, but her texts had become increasingly alarming. Her stepdad--"SD" as she called him--seemed to have lost it.

Monday: **SD cooked and ATE spiders for dinner. Got mad when mom and I refused to eat them. GROSS!!**

17

Tuesday: **SD now has 6 pet spiders. Gifts from Tod. They creep me out. Just like him. Asshole.**

Wednesday, 8:24 PM: **SD spending lotsa time in basement. Won't let mom or I go down. Such a jerkface.**

Wednesday, 10:11 PM: **Dunno what SD is up to, but I've been finding spiders all over. Killed three in my room 2nite. Afraid to sleep.**

Thursday: **SD and the Creep ate LIVE spiders tonite! Freak-ing GROSS!!!! Grabbed them out of a bowl and ate them like popcorn. Dozens of them. No idea where TOd's parents were. THey're zombies anyways. Idiots.**

Friday, 2:23 AM: **I snuck into the basement. Spiders everywhere. Just running around loose.**

Friday, 6:45 AM: **had it out w/ Dickhead abut baement. He said not 2 worry. I'd understand soon. Creepy, creepy. I'm starting to get scared, Uncle Ray.**

Friday, 3:44 PM: **Can't stand it anymore. SD going off about spiders and powr and how hes been chosen for te gift. Thinks hes Spider-man or somthin. Going to pond to read. Life Sux!!!**

Ray had stayed out of the picture this week, trying not to cause any more trouble for Amanda, but enough was enough. First, he'd find Amanda. Then he needed to have a chat with Shelly.

He drove up past her house and then past the Acres's house. The creepy kid lived in the sixth and last house, bordered by a wooded lot. As if empowered with some psychic sixth sense, there the kid stood in the driveway. Tod had his hands in his pockets again, and stood perfectly still. Unnaturally still for a kid his age. Ray shuddered. Seeing the freaky kid now made the skin between his shoulders tingle. Tod watched Ray until his car drove around the curve on the south side and headed back down the hill. Ray took a deep breath and let it out, feeling like a fool. Stupid kids. The things they'll do for effect.

The road formed a backwards "C" as it curled around. As the hill leveled out at the bottom, it headed northeast again. Whenever he came around that curve, he always dreaded what he might find. On one of the north lots, the builder had excavated a deep hole intended to become a basement before the guy had gone belly-up. So, now, the pit had become a stagnant pool and served as an ideal breeding ground for mosquitoes and frogs--a mud pit filled with clay-slip and slimy water. The town had filed an injunction to get the bank to fill it in, but the county, the bank, the creditors, and the investors were all arguing over whose responsibility it was. Last fall, during hunting season, a wounded deer had fallen in there and drowned. Ray had done his fair share of hunting as well, and he knew the value of deer hunting for keeping the tick population--and Lyme disease--in check. But he had no patience for incompetent hunters that wounded an animal and let it get away. It had taken a tow truck to haul it out and that had been fairly gruesome, even by his standards. Ray worried that some foolhardy kids or drunk teens would fall in and meet a similar fate.

And, typical of a rebellious fourteen year old, Amanda had chosen this as her favorite refuge. As expected, she sat in her usual spot, perched on the edge of the excavation with an eReader. He sighed. He'd talked to her about that numerous times. She was leaning against a 2x4, with one leg dangling into the basement area, kicking back and forth while she read.

She wore a white, mock turtleneck shirt with flowers on it and brown corduroy pants.

The width of the basement separated them. He walked up to the near side and called out to her. "Hello there, young lady."

She started, her arms and shoulders jerking upward.

Ray took off his hat and smiled, "Sorry. Didn't mean to surprise you." He gestured at a no trespassing sign with his hat. "You know you're not supposed to be here, right? It's not safe."

The girl looked at the sign and then back at him, playing along with their established routine. "So's going to high school, but they still make me go."

Ray gave her a chuckle. "Speaking of, I saw your buddy, Tod, on my way over."

That got her going. "He's not my buddy," she said in disgust. "He's a nutbag-jerk."

"Sounds like this whole spider obsession has gotten out of hand. Don't care for spiders myself," he added dryly.

Amanda giggled, putting a hand over her mouth. Ray's near-paralysis when it came to spiders was universally known throughout Braeburn, if not the county. He gazed eastward, pleased to have gotten a laugh. The woods along the undeveloped edge of the unfinished subdivision cast dense shadows in the gloomy gray light. The heavy pall sobered the moment.

"Do you want me to have a talk with your dad?"

She shook her head. "Nah." Her face looked alabaster pale under the gray sky. "I shouldnta bothered ya with my texts. Sorry." She looked at something behind him, over his left shoulder, and her eyes went wide with fear, and her already pale complexion turned white.

He turned in the direction she'd been looking and saw his truck--and, next to it, Tod Acres. His eyes were unnaturally large and black, which must have been a trick of the light. No one's eyes could be that large and that black. His face was a rictus of rage, his fists clenched and trembling by his side. The appearance of the boy and the clamped-down fury startled Ray.

"I...I have to go," she said and pulled her small frame up so fast, she slipped on the greasy clay edge of the pit, arms pinwheeling. Ray's heart pounded and his arms went out, even though the mucky water separated them, and he could not have helped her from where he stood. She gave him a half-wave and gathered her few belongings.

"You should stay away from Tod," she said. "He--" She broke off, eyes round. Without another word, she scurried away, back toward the houses up the hill.

"Hey, Amanda," he called after her, "Do me a favor, and stay off that ledge, okay?"

He turned his head to look at the boy again, but Tod Acres had disappeared. He saw only his Explorer, parked on the side of the road. The back of the hill rose ominously to the west of where he stood. Trees poked up as if from the balding head of a man buried up to his neck. On the other side of that hill, just out of sight, the strange boy in question did--what? Played? Schemed? More likely. Ray pursed his lips and shook his head in puzzlement at his niece's odd behavior.

He got back in the car and headed out of the subdivision. As he turned another curve, the sun flared into view, blinding him for a second; he stepped on the brake, unable to see. He flipped the visor down and found himself looking at four shiny eyes. Two metallic blue-black circles met his gaze in the center, and two smaller copper-bronze orbs on the outside edges. Bristly black and white hair covered the head and body of a spider. Metallic blue fangs gleamed in its mouth. The body was the size of a large grape. Ray saw all that in a tenth of a second. He slammed on the brake and jumped out of the vehicle, his arm getting momentarily tangled in the seat belt as he hopped backwards, the car door still open, his heart beating painfully against his ribs.

Son of a bitch! Damn and Double Damn! I hate spiders. I'd rather go into a burning building than face a big spider. Small spiders, no problem. Usually. Wasps, snakes, rats, bears, rabid raccoons--nothing else bothered him. But spiders? No thank you!

The car started to roll forward. He hadn't put it in park.

Shit!

He ran over to the car, grabbing the door and the frame and peered in, running along beside it. The Metallica Spider was nowhere to be seen. Shit! The thought of jumping into the car with the spider somewhere unseen filled him with dread, but explaining to the boys down at the firehouse how he'd wrecked his car was almost worse.

Shit! Shit! Shit!

Holding his breath, he jumped in.

He threw the car into park, but before he could jump out again, something moved angrily under his butt. Startled, he leaped off the seat. Even as he thought, in a panic, I'm sitting on the damn thing! Holy Shit! He scrambled sideways and fell out of the car and onto the road in an undignified heap.

Something buzzed in his back pocket again. His cell phone. Not a spider. It was his damned cell phone. He'd put it on vibrate mode during a meeting earlier today. With a sigh, he laid his head on the pavement and took the call. "This is Ray."

No one there. He dragged himself off the pavement and checked the ID. Missed call from Amanda. He tried to call her back, but it went to voicemail. He left a message and then leaned on the hood of his car and took a deep breath.

He stood outside the Explorer and peered in. He took another deep breath, closed his eyes for a half-second, opened them, exhaled. Wincing, he climbed into the car, closed the door, and put the car in drive. Gingerly, as if doing so might antagonize his guest, he pressed the gas pedal. He kept looking around, trying to find the damn spider, but he could not see anything.

As he exited the subdivision, he noticed dark shapes that looked like pears hanging in mid air. Thousands of dark fruit, blots on the heavy, overcast sky, moved up and down a network of threads that went from the power lines to the ground. He gaped, appalled at what he saw there. Spiders. Thousands of them, weaving, swaying and dropping toward the ground in the fall breeze. Ray drove east toward town and his body trembled.

As Ray pulled onto Route 31, he felt something on his neck. In a panic, he batted at it. Then he swore something had crawled up inside his pant leg, and he stomped his leg and slapped at his slacks as if they were on fire.

Before he even reached Main Street in town, sweat drenched his back and the armpits of his shirt. His thin hair clung to his head.

Ray picked up his mic and called Maggie Truman, the county dispatcher. "Maggie, this is Ray. Come in." Mags was tough-as-frozen-jerky and quick as a whip, so she could hand it right back to the guys when they tried to bust her chops.

"Ray, hey sugar. How're things in your neck of the woods?"

"I could use a beer, but since I'm on duty, I'll settle for a smoke. I'm stopping at the Wiggly. Need anything?"

"You sound stressed. What's going on? I thought you quit smoking," Maggie said.

"I did. Hey, any news on Ed yet?" he asked, changing the subject. Ed Johansson was the town's police chief, but he had written a note saying he'd be out of town for the next week and disappeared three days ago, without any further explanation. No other notice to his kids, his girlfriend, his mother, the town council, or his barber. No one had been able to reach him on his cell, either.

"Nope. No word yet, chief."

He started to tell her about the spiders on the telephone wires, but as he pulled into the Piggly Wiggly, he saw a scene of utter and complete chaos. Everyone he could see was either screaming or swearing or both. All across the lot, he saw people staring in dread from their cars or from the beds of their pickup trucks. One mother of three tossed her children into a truck like hay bails, swearing her head off the entire time.

Even Merle Evanston, a bouncer at the Silo Pub, and the meanest S.O.B. in town, was screaming like a little girl as he ran for his truck.

When he saw why he nearly passed out. As Ray watched, his worst nightmare appeared in front of him. A wave of spiders--fist-sized and furry--swarmed from out of nowhere and turned the black tar of the parking lot into the chocolate brown color of old canvas tents. Charlie Smothers, age five, fell to his hands and knees, as his mother ran ahead with his little sister. A particularly large spider used his head as a step and clambered up onto his back, continuing along with its trek west. Others crawled over his hands. For the rest of his life, Charlie would probably sleep with the light on.

Ray spotted the three elderly Weston siblings. Parker Weston dropped an entire case of champagne that he had special-ordered for their mother's 99th birthday next month, and the bottles burst, spraying out of the box in all directions. At 80 years old, he still managed to climb into the bed of a pickup truck like a teenager skipping school. The spiders, some as large as dinner plates, marched on unfazed. Audrey Weston, the youngest of the Westons at age 76, threw the same pickup truck into reverse, floored it, and slammed full on into the mayor's brand new Cadillac Escalade, almost throwing Parker over the side. Judy Weston was 79 years old. As Ray watched, her grocery bags slipped from her hands. A dozen eggs broke on the pavement, and Macintosh apples bounced across the parking lot; her eyes rolled up in her head, and she sank to the pavement like a dropped bathrobe. Her two siblings watched in dismay as the spiders continued to march over Judy's unconscious body. Each one ambled along, legs alternating like hairy fingers stretching out to steal an unwanted caress. They walked over her torso, clad in a modest blue dress, and across her bare legs--and over her face in their unceasing parade to the west. Toward the Sunnyside subdivision, Ray realized.

A shotgun erupted eliciting more screams and people ducking for cover. Merle Evanston had retrieved his shotgun from the rack in his truck and had blasted a Frisbee-sized spider back to hell. He fired off four more shots before he paused to reload the shotgun. Three other yahoos followed Merle's idiotic lead. Ray hoped no one would get killed from the ricochets.

A few moments later, the spiders were gone, disappeared into the woods on the far side of the lot. They left a weeping and gibbering mass of townsfolk collapsed in their wake.

Ray grabbed the first aid kit. Miraculously, only three people had been bitten--a small boy and two men, all of whom appeared to have swung at the spiders--but the toxins were creating severe reactions. Trouble breathing, rapid pulse, swelling, with severe pain pulsating outward from the bite site. Two others had been grazed by flying shotgun pellets, but nothing serious on that front. Ray figured they'd been lucky.

Ray recruited two off-duty nurses and some other folks to take the casualties to the medical clinic over in Calville.

As he watched the caravan head off, Brian Simmons bubbled away excitedly next to him. "THAT was amazing! I've never seen or even heard of a spider march that big before!"

Brian Simmons, a science teacher at the high school had helped stabilize the victims. Brian was a local legend of sorts. He was a science teacher at the high school and a spider fanatic. He'd been freaking kids and townsfolk out with his presentations since he got hired a few years back. If he was game, he might be useful.

"You mean they actually do that? This?" Ray said, appalled and waved his arm around at the parking lot.

"Oh, yeah. They march for breeding. It's rare, though, and never this far north--or this big a group. Just fantastic."

"Ugh. Great. So what kind were they?"

"That's the thing. I don't know." His pudgy kid-like face broke into a big, ecstatic grin. "And I should! I'm president of the Illinois Arach-Nuts Club. There's not a spider in North America I don't know." He held up his camera, "And I've got pictures! I've already got a title, 'The Great Spider March of 2013.'" He got a dreamy look on his face, the way Ray used to get when he thought about Marlene McGillan back in eighth grade.

Ray shook his head, dumbfounded that anyone would be even remotely interested in spiders, much less enough to join a club about 'em. "Well, I know where they're headed, I think, and I'm going out there now. If you'd like to tag along, I could use your insights." And an extra pair of eyes to keep the spiders off my neck, he added to himself.

"How do you know where they're off to?"

"A very strong hunch."

Brian got into Ray's SUV. Ray hesitated to get in. With no small amount of trepidation, Ray looked in his SUV for his eight-legged companion from earlier.

"Problem?" Brian asked.

"No, no problem," Ray replied. Not seeing the hitchhiker, Ray got in and headed west, back toward the Sunnyside development. He needed to find out where the heck these spiders were headed before more people got hurt.

Mags called him on the radio. "Justine Barstow had a heart attack. Her husband said she went out to get the mail and when she turned around, a mass of spiders had cut her off from the house. They just walked right over her. By the time they were gone, she was dead. Barney's on his way over there now." Barney Harris was the county coroner. Ray filled Maggie in on what happened at the Wiggly while he drove. Ray turned the corner at the end of Main Street and headed west on County Road 31.

"Be careful, Ray. I saw on TV some of these spider bites can kill the skin. Like permanently. And the dead part just expands and expands like a Danish or something." She popped her gum into the mic, making Ray jump and swerve the car.

"Whoa!" Brian yelled and clutched at the armrest.

"Dammit, Mags! I've asked you not to do that. And thanks for the visual. Its called necrosis, and I'll probably never be able to eat another Danish."

"Glad I could help your cholesterol, boss." She snapped her gum again. "Maggie out."

He could hear the smile in her voice and sighed.

As they pulled into Sunnyside, they looked up at the "Welcome to Sunnyside" sign. Brian pointed out a pie-sized spider covering up the "W", making Ray feel slightly nauseous. Then Brian spotted the spiders hanging from the telephone and electrical wires.

"No way! Pull over, pull over!"

Of average height, Simmons was still a large man, perhaps from eating too many necrotic Danishes. He wore khakis and a midnight-blue button shirt with a subtle black pattern on it. He had short, neatly cut hair that nevertheless hung down over his eyes. He brushed it aside distractedly, and started snapping off pictures with a long-lens camera.

"Isn't this amazing?!" Simmons said.

Ray unfolded his long body from the car and shuddered as he got out. "Yeah. Can't say it'll do much for property values, though."

Simmons missed the comment, too caught up in the spectacle before him. "I've never seen this breed of spider before. This one is even different from the one at the Wiggly. New species are being discovered all the time, though, but usually in remote places. Last year, they discovered five new species."

He pointed to the scores of spiders spinning webs from the lines. "I've only seen that in Brazil." He gave him a sheepish grin, "Well, I've seen it on YouTube. I've never been to Brazil. You?"

"I don't like traveling." He thought, but did not say, too many bugs.

Brian looked through his lens again and said, "The spiders on the telephone lines appear to be the same species as at the Wiggly. Can't be sure though without a closer look."

"Well, here come the migrating ones now." Ray nodded his head back to the turnoff from Route 31 into Sunnyside. The army of arachnida creeped across the road. Brian snapped off pictures as fast as his camera would allow. A green mini-Cooper slammed on the brakes to avoid driving over the bizarre crossing.

If they had gone straight west, they would have skirted along the southern edge of the Sunnyside property. That would have been the natural flow, based on their trend so far. This time, however, instead of staying the course, the spiders followed the curve of the road, straight for them.

"Shit!" Ray said and ran for the Explorer.

"Hey," Brian yelled. "Where are you going? They won't hurt you. This is historic, man."

"I've got three people on the way to the clinic who'd say otherwise."

Ray watched, appalled, as Brian crouched down and took photos at ground level and then took more photos standing up as the invaders surrounded him and crawled over his brown leather shoes. He shuddered as he watched, and he could taste bile in his throat.

Ray stared in horrified fascination, unable to close his eyes or even look away. He hated the fact that he could not see the ones that passed under his SUV. Hated not knowing if they kept going or if some of them decided to stop and set up shop in the undercarriage of his car. Not that he had any inclination to get out and look. He watched in horrid loathing as the creepy-crawly little bastards inched along like dismembered but still animated hands. They were brown and grey striped, with black bands, and as hairy as the Methodist choir director's legs in the middle of winter.

Ray, sitting in the car alone, said, "They say idle hands are the devil's workshop. Seems to me that the busy ones are more of a problem at the moment." He looked in the rearview mirror at his haunted face. "Great. Now I'm talking to myself, and I look crazy, too."

It took twenty minutes for the parade to pass by, a river of the creatures Ray hated most in the universe. When the last of them meandered up the hill and disappeared toward the weird kid's house, Ray raised a trembling hand and wiped the sweat off his brow as Brian got in the car, gushing like a football fan during playoffs.

"Did you see that big one toward the front? It must have been as big as a tire! Amazing!"

"You're sick. Has anyone ever told you that? Sick."

The man chuckled. "My students tell me that all the time. I love spiders! C'mon, let's follow the marching band."

Ray shook his head, but he put the car in drive and started up the hill. The clouds had peeled back from the horizon, and the setting sun was blinding as day drew to a close, so the fire chief flipped down his visor and that's when it happened--again.

He caught a glimpse of the metallic spider as it spilled down from the sunscreen. He tried to bat at it as the pesky thing fell, but it bounced off his arm and right into the opening of his button-down shirt.

Ray's voice rose an octave as he beat at his chest like a man trying to give himself CPR, which he figured wasn't far off. He had never been more religious than at that moment. "Oh, Jesus, Jesus! Get it off me! Oh, Christ!"

For the second time that day he jumped out of a moving car. He whipped up his shirt bottom and shook it like a sail in the Americas Cup. He pulled the shirt over the top of his head and practically whimpered when his hands got caught in the cuffs. He whipped his arms around and, when that didn't work, he stepped on the offending shirt and pulled until his hands popped free.

He looked over and saw Brian sitting in the driver's seat and staring at him with round eyes.

"What?" Ray snapped.

"Nothing," Brian said, his voice a careful study in casualness. He put the car in park and stepped out of the vehicle.

Ray picked up his shirt and shook it. A spider fell out and landed on the pavement.

Brian flipped it over with a pencil and said, "Ah, Phidippus audax. The bold jumping spider. Never seen one this big before, though. Harmless, really. Very pretty chelicerae."

"What?"

"Mouth parts. These metallic green parts that look like fangs. The fangs are in there, but they're actually much smaller."

"Very reassuring. Come on." He yanked his shirt on, ignoring the few missing buttons, and got back in, slamming the door shut. Brian moved his larger bulk around the front of the car with surprising speed and got back in.

He waited until Brian buckled in and then punched the gas, burning rubber. "Look," he growled, knowing he was being unreasonable, but not caring at the moment. "No more science crap, okay? I just want to check on my cousin and her daughter and find out what the hell the damn spiders are doing and get out of here."

"Uh, okay. Sure."

The spiders came to the veer-off that Ray had followed a few hours ago. Instead of going straight, as one would reasonably have expected, that being the path of least resistance, they turned right. Toward Tod Acres' house. And toward Amanda's house. Although it made no rational sense, some part of Ray was not surprised.

Although they could have easily climbed over them, the curbs channeled the spiders, and kept them mostly on the road. On the right side, the land sloped off in a hill that led to a band of trees too thin to be called a woods before opening out into another street empty of houses down below. The left side had empty lots sparsely populated with weeds. Ray cranked the wheel hard left and jumped the curb. He gunned it, spraying up clods of dirt and stones that pummeled the undercarriage.

"Whoa!" Brian yelled for the second time and grabbed on to the handle as he was bounced around like a stuffed sandy-blonde bear.

Ray hit a large spider that had wandered off the road and onto the dirt lot. "Splat," he said and laughed. He gave Brian a big smile.

The fire chief off-roaded it past the three empty houses, then past the burned out ruin, popped over the crest of the hill and onto the manicured lawn of Amanda Harding's house and plowed directly into a sea of overly large tarantulas. A wave of spiders was leaving the road and swarming into the Harding's rural dream home. Ray hit dozens of them, and they made a sound like squelching mud. He cranked the wheel and the Explorer slammed into a tree. Spiders ranging in size from baseballs to medium pizzas fell to the hood and roof with dull thuds. One landed on the windshield and raised its front legs, hissing. Ray hit the windshield wipers and knocked it off the glass.

He'd more than half-expected the spiders to leave the road, but at the same time thought he was crazy for even thinking it, and he'd expected them at the next house over, at the Acres', not here at Amanda's house. That would have been bad enough. Thinking of his young niece in there with this eerie wave of spiders was much, much worse.

All the windows of the home were open, as well as the front door and the garage. The spiders flowed inside, shambling eastward now, like a waterfall running in reverse. Ray thought he might be sick.

"Son of a bitch," he said. He rested his forehead on the steering wheel and closed his eyes for a moment.

"You okay?" Brian wore a worried expression, as if he feared he might have to give Ray CPR or something.

"Yeah. Peachy. Okay, Spider-man. Let's go."

Brian raised his eyebrows. "Go?"

"Yes. Go. My cousin and her daughter--my niece-- are in there." He jabbed an angry finger at the house, as if it were the house's fault. Ray swallowed and finished his sentence. "We're going in."

"Cousin and niece? Is that some sort of rural someone-married-their-sister thing?" Brian asked.

The question didn't fully register with Ray. He was focused on getting out of the Ford. He opened his door with trepidation, nerves in hyperdrive, but the spiders had cleared away from the truck's sudden appearance. He went around back, his skin crawling, eyes scanning the tree above in constant paranoia of a spider dropping on his head like a scene from *Aliens*. He put on his bunker gear--pants, jacket, boots, as well as his Nomex hood, his gloves, and his helmet. He handed Brian an axe and a fire extinguisher and picked up a long multi-tool and a second fire extinguisher for himself.

"What is that thing?" Brian asked.

"Halligan bar. Axe, hammer, and pry bar all in one."

Brian looked at him, his face barely stifling a smirk. "Aren't you a tad overdressed?"

"I'm not taking any chances with these eight-legged bastards. Let's go." He stepped over a tarantula, his stomach doing a little flip, and then flicked aside a group of three more to make a stepping spot. Working as quickly as possible without pissing off the spiders any more than necessary, they made their way to the front door.

They went in and paused for a moment, simply watching, taking it all in. Ray could not believe the transformation that had taken place in Tim and Shelly's home in such a short time. It seemed utterly impossible to him. Thick nests of white silk hid under tables and in corners in the room off to the right and in the hallway that stretched out straight ahead of them, leading to the living room just visible further back. Webs stretched from the chandelier overhead to the second floor walkway that went perpendicular to the ground floor hallway where they stood. Ray knew that the open passage above connected the bedrooms on the left and right side of the house. More white luminous sacks clung to the walkway up overhead, overripe and evil nests. As a firefighter, Ray kept his bearings instinctively. East lay straight ahead, toward the back of the house; the road was behind them to the west.

The spiders they could see moved in an unending stream into the first floor, flowing somewhere toward the family room in the back, the office and the basement. With a glance at each other, they followed the grim procession. If they had walked into the room on the right, a basically unused sitting room, and seen the funnel-shaped nest in the corner, out of sight from the entryway, they might have avoided tragedy. Instead, they moved further into the house.

Ray's skin tingled with spasming nerves as they stepped under the open hallway and into the family room and kitchen area. The living room opened up from the first floor up to the second with a vaulted ceiling. A set of stairs parallel to the front of the house went up to an open hallway that looked down from the walkway overhead. East of the kitchen, they could see through a sliding glass door and onto a deck. Ray knew from summer barbeques that stairs led down to a small backyard and another sliding glass door into the walkout basement.

Ray and Brian watched a moment while the spiders flowed north and then back west before disappearing into the basement stairwell.

Although Ray wanted to see what the spiders were doing, he needed to find his family first. They turned left and went up the staircase that hugged the wall on the west side and opened out into the room on the east. Ray could imagine kids tossing paper airplanes into the room from their various stalking points along the stairs. No longer. Those spindles were the perfect haven for web-spinners, and now threads and sheets of gossamer took over the railing.

"What the hell happened here?" Brian asked.

Ray grunted. "What the hell is still going on here?"

Donald J. Hunt

"There are at least five species of spiders I've never seen in Illinois before."

Ray didn't respond. When they reached the landing on top, the master bedroom lay off to the south, which was now on his left, and across the walkway. Amanda's bedroom was closer, but the master bedroom door was open most of the way, and they had a clear view. At the sight on the bed, Ray let out a low and an involuntary, "No," which sounded more moan than spoken word.

A mutant, giant silk cocoon domed up over the bed. The two men moved forward with slow, reluctant steps. The dense, sick-sweet smell of death clung to the room like the spider webs all around them. Ray pointed at a human foot with a tattooed ankle just outside the web. A thick, well-knotted rope secured it to the Shaker-style footboard. They could see ropes through the gauzy webs at all four corners of the bed. Ray recognized the butterfly and thorn tattoo as Shelly's. He remembered when she'd gotten the tattoo at sixteen, and there had been hell to pay with her folks. He also recalled playing around the creek by their grandparents' house one time when she'd grabbed hold of some roots to climb up the bank--and a large hairy brown-gray spider had climbed out of the dark and onto her forearm. She'd screamed and wet her pants. Shelly and Ray had shared a loathing of spiders ever since.

Despite the grisly scene, he stepped into the room. He had to know. Even though she had to be dead, he still had to know.

With his second step forward, an orange-yellow shape the size of a football and with multiple flailing legs

38

darted out from the side near the door and attacked Ray's leg. It felt like a kid knuckle-punching his Kevlar-reinforced pants. He leaped backward, back into the hall, and fell over, dropping his fire extinguisher. He knocked the spider off his leg with his Halligan bar and it raised its front legs, readying for another charge.

Brian's axe cut it in half and it twitched on the floor. His breath came in and out in ragged breath. "African Trapdoor spider of some sort. Unusually large. Not usually so aggressive." He gave Ray a weak smile and gestured into the room. "After you."

They reached the head of the bed without another attack. Shelly was, thankfully, dead. Dozens of spider babies crawled around her face and in and out of her gaping mouth. She looked like she had died terrified. Ray could relate.

He heard a retching noise and turned to see Brian gagging and holding his hand over his mouth. He turned to go back into the hall. Ray made to follow after, his mind numb with shock and grief. Childhood memories crowded his thoughts, making it hard to focus. Even so, he noted in a distracted way several other bundles of silk around the room and wondered if they were egg sacks or spider traps. Brian, his stomach roiling, stumbled and grabbed the edge of the door. Ray, behind him, saw something move, but his reactions were off, too slow. The science teacher screamed and ran into the hall. He flung his arm around like a man on fire, and a spider, easily as wide as Ray's hand with fingers extended, landed on the ground and charged after the large man, legs flying like a professional typist. It pounced on Brian's leg and tore ferociously at his pants. Not wanting to bash Brian's legs with his multi-tool, Ray turned the fire extinguisher on the arachnid to blast it off. As he did, he caught a good look at it. The thing was another walking freak show. The front of its body gleamed black like a freshly waxed car. The abdomen, by contrast looked like a flat-black leather baseball, but shaped like a poisonous kiwi. As if sensing him, it turned, jumped off Brian, and took a challenging leap at Ray. The fire chief triggered the fire extinguisher and held his Halligan bar out in front of him like a spear. Blasted backward and covered in foam, the spider skittered over the edge of the walkway and disappeared.

Brian moaned and cradled his arm.

"Let me see your arm."

Brian held it out. "Nothing you can do. Some type of Australian Funnel Spider. Fatal without antivenin. None around here. Musta been a nest." He closed his eyes and grimaced. "Behind the door."

Ray saw that the arm had been ravaged. Six bites that he could see, with bright red welts. He checked Brian's leg; the pant leg and hiking boot had been ripped and torn as if by a jagged knife, but it had not gotten through to the skin.

"Jesus." Ray pulled a strap off of his utility belt and quickly tied a tourniquet around Brian's arm. "How fast is the poison?" he asked.

"Half an hour. Maybe four days." He bit his lip. "Give or take. Funnel guys...bite through shoes."

"Yeah, I see that. Let's get you to the clinic. They can FedEx it overnight."

He groaned. "Shit, man. Burns. Blood is pounding."

"That's the tourniquet."

Brian swallowed thickly. "Spider's not local," he repeated between rapid, shallow breaths. "Owner might have antivenin." He swallowed again. "Fridge."

Ray hesitated. If they went back downstairs, they'd lose valuable time. He picked a bare spot on the wall and told Brian, "Sit here. I've got to look for Amanda before we go back down."

"Not alone."

"Yes, alone." Ray said firmly. "You sit. I'll just be a minute." Before Brian could argue more, Ray took off.

Amanda's bedroom was dark, heavy curtains drawn. Holding his breath, Ray hit the light switch. The room blazed into light, sending some spiders skittering, while others held their ground. None of them charged him, thankfully. His nerves sang like an out of tune piano in a church basement. He checked Amanda's bedroom, the guest room, and a bathroom. He found no new victims.

When he came back out into the hall, Brian had worked his way into a standing position, and he held the axe in his good hand, but sweat covered his head and darkened the armpits of his shirt. Ray picked up the second fire extinguisher, and they headed downstairs.

Ray and Brian stuck to the middle, heads jerking this way and that in reaction to movements, real and imagined. They did not see the funnel spider, but that did not reassure either of them very much.

In one of his glances, Ray looked through the twilight gloom overtaking the great room and saw the cherubic form of Tod Acres stepping out of the first floor office. Unreasonable rage filled him. He did not knowing what, exactly, he suspected the kid of having done--for how could he possibly be involved with something that had caused all this? At least in the sane, rational world Ray had lived in only yesterday, there was no way a child could have been involved in something so surreal. Ray charged down the last few steps and after the kid. He felt a spider squish under his booted foot and cringed; he ignored the sensation. Plenty of time to be sick later.

The boy startled upright at Ray's sudden movement, eyes wide "O"s of surprise, and then he bolted for the sliding glass door at the back of the eating area. The chief grabbed the kid by the shirt and spun him around.

He had planned to demand answers, but the boy's eyes had changed to round, black baseballs. Impossible, unfathomable, onyx orbs framed in a face of hate. The thing opened its mouth and the fangs--not fangs, Brian had said; cholera-something-or-other--of a spider quivered within. Black, fleshy and hairy protuberances hung down, reminiscent of a walrus' upper lip, with smooth black curves that sprouted from that bristled, jutting flesh, and sure as shit looked like fangs to Ray. Tod Acres hissed and lunged at him, and Ray fell over backwards onto the floor as he backpedalled away in fear.

The door flew open and the mutant boy-slash-spider was gone. As Ray got up, he saw that the little creep had dropped a book. A quick flip through the book revealed it to be a diary, but he'd have to read it later. He slipped it into his pocket.

The fire chief turned back and saw Brian leaning against the fridge, eyes closed, breathing heavily. He'd clearly missed whatever the hell had just happened.

"Brian," he said. The large man opened his eyes. Ray looked a question at him, and did a head bob toward the fridge. Brian shook his head. No antivenin. Sweat beaded the man's face and dampened his blond-brown hair. He cradled his injured arm.

Ray's phone rang. He had taken it off vibrate, and it sounded shrill in the silent spider mausoleum. He looked at the caller ID and answered the phone. "Amanda! Where are you?" Ray said.

He heard her voice, tinny and distorted, as if far away, interspersed with silence. "Uncle.......the basement. Oh, God! Please....... it's....... my dad.......it.......mons......." For a moment, he thought he heard banging and scraping, but then he lost the connection completely.

He heard more scraping and banging and took another look at the phone. No connection. Then he realized the sound came from the basement.

He looked at Brian. "Go. Go!" Brian waved his uninjured arm. "Right behind you." He threw himself upright, off the fridge he had been leaning on, with obvious effort to show Ray he could make it. He waved his hand to emphasize the message. Go ahead.

Ray headed for the basement door. He wanted to go faster, but even if Brian hadn't been injured, he couldn't. There were simply too many damned spiders in the way. He moved through them like a kid shuffling through leaves in the fall and felt, once again, slightly queasy as he did so. When one of the spiders--a brilliant orange thing with black bands--started to crawl up his leg, he did not realize he had been whimpering until after he'd knocked it off with the base of his fire extinguisher.

As he reached the top of the basement stairs, Ray heard a sound like a bookcase being dragged and then more of that odd banging, as if someone were hitting a full metal garbage can. As Brian caught up to him, he hit the light switch to the basement and they heard a whispering noise and then silence. They waded down the basement staircase, which ran parallel to the road out front. Ray used his booted feet to brush the knotted mass of spiders off the creaky wooden steps in quick sweeps, again feeling his gorge rise. At the bottom, the pale light of a single low wattage bulb hung down from an electric cord looped over a pipe--a safety violation, the fire chief noted in passing; it swung slightly as if troubled by a breeze and revealed a perditious scene.

A man in black robes lay on the floor, blood on his arm, face and chest. Ray took a second look and recognized Tim Harding's face, but what he saw shocked him. The thirty-something year old had painted his forehead with very realistic spider eyes as well drawing curved mouthparts on his long, bony visage. His painted face emulated the grotesquery that Tod Acres had recently revealed.

The size of the bite marks added to Ray's growing dread. It looked like someone stuck a damned harpoon in him.

Ray had been well-trained to look for danger before going in to help someone and, despite his revulsion, his instinct was still to try and help Tim. Ray scanned the scene. Spiders of all shapes and sizes crawled all around the man but, eerily, did not climb on or near him. The acrid and cloying smell of something burned and pungent pricked at his firefighter's senses. He spotted black candles toppled nearby, and a circle had been inscribed on the floor with strange symbols or letters he did not recognize. Some kind of cult-circle, or whatever the hell these nuts called those things.

The basement windows were choked with sheet webs. The rafters overhead rippled with cobwebs and tent webs. God, he wished he had not looked overhead. Spiders hung above them by the score, upside down spectators and specters to the scene they observed below. He could feel their multiple eyes upon him as they considered whether or not he was prey.

Off to the right, toward the south side of the room, beyond Tim's unconscious body, an old rusty and dented fridge lay on its back, looking like a pastel green coffin. Straight ahead of the fridge, he saw a sliding glass door for the walkout basement, which is precisely what he wanted to do now. Walk. The Hell. Out. To the far right, beyond the fridge, he could see workbenches, Bunsen burners, racks with frames in them, and piles of boxes in the moldering dim light. And more spiders shifting around in the dim murkiness. Of course.

Ray looked to the left, past the staircase they had descended, and he almost passed out. A cinder block wall went up to chest height; from there, a crawl space should have gone back under the rest of the house, with a fifteen or twenty foot wide opening. Instead, on either side someone had cemented cobblestones, random rocks, brick and debris into the wall. The opening was now perhaps five feet by five feet, and it was covered in the dense cyclone shape of a funnel web.

"Ray! There's somebody in here!" He tore his eyes away from the horrid lair and saw Brian yanking on the handle of the mangled fridge. "It's jammed."

"Amanda!" Ray raced over, slipping on some vials and packets that lay scattered on the floor in front of it. He joined in and they both pulled, but the door would not budge. He could hear a feeble beating from within and knew that she must be running out of air by now.

Ray grabbed his Halligan and said, "Watch out." He swung the tool like an axe. Sparks flew from the metal, and on the second blow, the latch clunked to the floor. They pulled the door up and helped Amanda up and out of the container as she gasped for breath.

"Had to hide." Deep gasp. "Tried to kill me. My stepdad." Another gasp. "I couldn't get out the door." She gestured at the sliding glass door of the walkout basement. She started to cry at that memory, and he wrapped his arms around her shoulders. Another deep, shuddering breath.

"Easy. Slow down." He held her out at arms' length.

As her breath came more easily, so did the words. "He tied my wrists. But not my feet. He had a knife, and he made me kneel down. Tod started chanting in some strange language and walking around the circle, with us in it, and the spiders everywhere." She bit at her fist as if trying to fight back terror with pain, which perhaps she was. "Tod was waving this lantern-thingy with a horrible

46

smelling smoke coming from it. And when I looked in his face, I saw--I saw--"

But she couldn't finish the sentence any more than Ray could volunteer what he'd seen. Not there. Not then. "Easy. Easy does it," Ray said again.

"I heard something crack, super loud, like the house broke, you know, or a mountain? And then a gust of hot air with strange smells, like Aunt Muriel's spice cabinet all mixed up with a dried up scummy pond. Tim...he looked into the crawlspace and I jumped up and kneed him." A hint of a smile touched her lips at that.

"I grabbed the knife and ran, but I couldn't get out the door," she said again. "Locked. Tod kept chanting, louder and faster, and Tim was getting up, pissed, you know? So I dumped the stuff out of the fridge and climbed in. I pulled the door shut, and I thought, 'If I can just call Uncle Ray, I'll have a chance.'"

"They kept banging on the fridge. Flipping it over. I thought I was going to die." She looked into her uncle's eyes. "I was so scared," she whispered.

"And incredibly brave," Ray said.

Ray looked over at the crawl space. He knew, without a doubt, that something lurked in there, waiting.

Still peering into the dark funnel, for a brief moment, too quickly for him to even cry out, within those layers of webbing, Ray saw the sheen of polished black stones, numerous orbs the size of fists. He noted with numb, unholy terror that they were in a setting of bristled hairs. Eyes? Were they eyes?! Looking at him, marking him. Unblinking eyes--but larger than a spider's eyes, impossibly larger. Much, much larger. Surely, they could not be a spider's eyes? But then, the opening of the funnel, at the point where it drove deeper inward, stood maybe three feet wide. And then, so fast he thought perhaps he had imagined it all, they disappeared, lost in that labyrinth of web.

He took an involuntary step forward, trying to see, unable to believe that he could possibly be seeing what he thought he was seeing. Moving his hand slowly, Ray reached up and flicked on his helmet light. The piercing light could not completely penetrate the woven silk.

Within that shadowy lair, they heard a noise like a giant madman scribbling furiously on parchment with an oversized pencil, and then the clamor shifted to a repetitive thrumming that brought to mind his grandmother working away on her old foot-powered sewing machine. The thrumming ended in an emphatic thunk as if a heavy wooden cabinet door clicked shut, making the three of them jump.

After a moment's pause, a different noise began, and this last set of noises chilled his blood. An emphatic tapping that sounded like some bizarre and alien version of Morse code--overlapping and arrhythmic--started up. The unnatural sound grated against and disturbed the mind. When the sounds stopped, they waited, both grateful and yet frozen in terror, waiting to see if the perpetrator of such an incongruous bedlam would show itself. Instead, the whole pattern repeated again.

The spiders gathered on the floor below the crawl space raised quivering front legs toward the opening. Dozens and dozens of them, all facing that silken funnel, and all in the same posture, as if giving homage to a liege lord or praying to a god.

He shook his head and came back to himself, as if from some sort of drugged daze or hypnotic episode, that Amanda clutched at his arm. He knew he should be doing something, but his shocked brain wouldn't work, couldn't process all this. He moved in a numb catatonia.

"We really need to get out of here," Brian said.

"Yeah," Ray said. "Yeah. Help me with Tim." He could make sure he was stable after they got the hell out of here. Screw protocol.

He took a step closer to that gauze-covered murk, preparing to pick up Tim's shoulders, but he'd have to go closer to that fetid pit, and then turn his back on it to lift him. Good God, how could he do it? He was just considering dragging Tim away from the area by his ankles when Ray once more thought he caught a glimpse of movement within that unnatural chamber. There! An object shiny and black and goddamn huge!

It shifted out of view, disappearing yet again, and Ray shuffled backwards a couple of steps.

"Did you--" but when he turned to Brian, the larger man was scrabbling and tossing aside vials and packets on the floor, looking for the antivenin. Amanda nodded, bone-pale under the bare incandescent bulb, mouth pressed into a thin, downward curve.

Ray whipped his head back around and he imagined he could see coarse hairy limbs shifting in the impenetrable gloom. He would have sworn he saw the glassy alienness of a spider's eyes glittering at him.

49

Keeping a wary eye on the opening to the crawl space, Ray slid forward once more. Leaving the fire extinguishers over by Brian, he moved next to Tim, and set the Halligan next to him.

Ray set aside his revulsion and checked for a pulse and breathing. Freak's alive? Check. Pulse racing, breathing labored. The wounds appeared to be insect bites, swollen and bright red, but the size of the punctures made it look like he'd been stabbed with a screwdriver instead of a bite. Tim did not stir, but he seemed stable enough to move.

"Okay, Amanda, you'll have to help me. Brian's been--"

Amanda suddenly screamed and Ray ducked instinctively and staggered away from the crawlspace. He glanced behind him. Something the size of a small car, black and hairy with glass eyes and articulated legs stabbed and gnashed its way toward him. There was no way he could grab the pry bar, so he did the only thing he could. He screamed and scrabbled away from the thing as quickly as he could.

Paralysis gripped his mind, and he watched in horror as the creature--far too large to be called just a spider--snatched up Tim Harding from the floor with its front legs and with terrifying speed reversed course and dragged the man back into its den. His right leg and shoe caught on the lip, but then disappeared with a final tug. Ray backed up until he bumped into Amanda.

A fresh round of panic-sweat popped out all over his body. He suppressed a whimper for Amanda's sake, and Ray pushed her gently but insistently toward the sliding glass door. "Go!" he said. Inside, his mind screamed in near-hysteria. Go, go, go! Get out. Gotta get out. Out. Gotta get out. Gotta get away from here.

Unwilling to leave behind his only weapon, his Halligan bar, he stepped forward and stretched out his fingers with great trepidation toward that preternatural beast. Just before he grasped the pry bar, noises started coming from the crawl space again and he jerked his hand back in reflexive panic. An insistent and urgent alien staccato punctuated the air and dust sifted down from the rafters overhead. The spiders crowded closer to the crawl space, although none presumed to scale the wall.

Then, as one, the spiders turned toward Ray, Brian and Amanda. Ray lunged out, grabbed the Halligan bar from the floor and ran.

"Time to go," Brian said and they joined Amanda at the basement's sliding glass door. It would not budge. Harding had nailed it shut. As one, Ray swung the Halligan and Brian swung the axe at the glass wall before them. The glass turned opaque in a parody of spider webs that mocked their efforts to escape, but then crashed to the ground when they kicked at the glass. Amanda went first, then Brian. Ray turned and looked behind him and saw the entire room of spiders shift toward them.

"Shit!" he said, his voice higher than normal.

"What?" Brian yelled over his shoulder.

"Just run!"

Ray and Amanda grabbed Brian's arms, helping him stumble along. They ran outside and to the left, up a grass slope with a brick walled off storage area between them and the house. They dodged stray spiders who apparently hadn't received their marching orders yet.

When they reached the truck over toward the side of the front yard, Ray pointed north as he yanked open the back.

"Go to the burned out house next door. I'll meet you there in a few minutes."

"What? What are you doing?" Amanda said, her voice awash with hysteria.

In answer, Ray pulled out one of the two cans he kept for running generators. He spun off the front and back caps and poured one of the cans down the hill where the spiders were coming at them. Reaching into a pocket, he pulled out a pack of matches. Only one. Damn. He ripped off the cardboard match and lit the book on fire. He tossed it on the gasoline flowing downhill, and the encroaching spiders, went up with a whoosh! The spiders make a crackling noise as they burned and shriveled in on themselves.

"Go on!" he yelled at Brian and Amanda. They didn't argue but instead took off running.

Fortunately, the brick storage area kept the house from catching fire as well. Even a fast house fire would not suffice for the hellspawn Ray had seen in the basement.

He stuffed a rag in the second can. He knew he did not have much time. Whatever that was in the basement was issuing orders. He climbed into the cab, popped the lighter in, and gunned the engine toward the front of the house, heedless of the spider bodies crunching under his tires.

The lighter popped as he pulled up to the open front door. He considered lighting and throwing his Molotov cocktail in, but had another idea. He pushed the lighter back in to keep it hot, grabbed the Halligan, and ran inside the house, his nerves jangling from repeated fear-reactions. He ran to the kitchen and cranked up all the burners on the stove; but he knew even with all four going full tilt, it would take too long for the gas to spread.

He ran into the laundry room, over by the garage-- and the stairs going down, which he did not want to think about. He pulled the dryer away from the wall. He was in luck. Gas, not electric. He grabbed the mini-bolt cutters off his tool belt, murmured a prayer, squinted, and cut the gas line.

He was still there, so the house hadn't blown up. Yet.

He hurried from the room, past the kitchen and under the walkway. He was heading for the door when someone tapped him insistently, angrily on the shoulder.

His blood froze. No one else is here! screamed in his brain. He beat at his shoulder in panic and a black spider flew off and into the hallway wall. Ray recognized the odd mix of shiny and flat black on its body--the Australian Funnel Spider that bit Brian. Shit! It charged back at him, moving incredibly fast. It slammed into his leg and tore at his boot like a bulldog. Not having luck chewing through the Kevlar, it turned its head, and black-glass eyes stared into Ray's own eyes. It launched for his face, climbing up his body like a tree. Ray shrieked and, waving his arm wildly, flung it aside, more by luck than anything. It landed on its back, but flipped over and rounded, advancing on him yet again with blazing speed. Before it could leap at him, though, Ray, crazed with fear-adrenalin screamed a challenge of his own and charged. He swung the pry-bar end of the Halligan like a golf club. The spider flew backwards, bounced off the front door and lay still on the oriental carpet. Ray didn't pause. He swung the multi-tool around and slammed the spike through the thing's body. Terror channeled into rage, he kept swinging the pike end, the curved steel biting through the spider and into the hardwood floor beneath. He had to wrench it loose after each blow.

"Sonuva..."

Thunk!

"Goddamn..."

Thunk!

"Bitch..."

Thunk!

With the last blow, and to make sure it was dead, he rotated the tool and brought the hammerhead down on it, turning it into a flattened mess. He stood up, breathing hard and looked back into the hallway. A cascade of spiders moved toward him.

Ray ran outside, slamming the door shut. He grabbed the lighter from its socket in the dash, and held it to the rag, but it would not catch. It had cooled off already. Ray laughed, a mad, frenzied sound. "Of course!" He pushed in the lighter and rocked back and forth in the seat as he waited for it to heat back up. "Comeon-comeon-comeon," he said, fresh beads of sweat covering his forehead. He watched, captivated, as spiders attempted to climb out of the open windows, while others, newcomers who had not yet received the latest order to kill Ray Canfield, still attempted to scurry into the house.

The lighter popped out and Ray let out a little sob of relief. He drove the car in front of the window, lit the rag, the flames dancing dangerously close to his face, and hurled the can in like a medicine ball, shattering the glass. He did a 180-degree turn in the front lawn and pressed the pedal to the floor, churning up grass and dirt. He was unaware that he giggled, laughed, and wept as the vehicle bucked its way off the Harding property.

The house erupted into a column of fire as he picked up Brian and Amanda at the house next door.

Winter had come and gone. Spring had arrived for its traditional day or two and then turned into a blazing hot summer, which had rolled back around to fall again. The townsfolk had moved on with their lives, but one could not say things had gotten back to normal.

The two elderly men bitten at the Piggly Wiggly had ended up dying, although the boy had lived. Brian also lived, thanks to the antivenin he had found in the basement. But necrosis set in, despite chemical treatments, surgery, and even maggot treatments to remove the dead skin. Secondary infections had set in and, in the end, his arm had to be amputated. He and Ray had become friends and got together every week or so now. Brian was still an expert on spiders, even more so now, perhaps, but he no longer gushed enthusiastically about the eight-legged bastards.

With both of Amanda's parents dead, and no other relatives, she had become Ray's responsibility and they'd turned a spare room into her bedroom. Amanda had later told him that she'd seen Tod Acres by Ray's truck that day, but she'd been afraid to say anything. He'd glared and pointed at her from behind Ray's truck, and she'd panicked. Tod could be quite...cruel...if he chose to be. She'd regretted running as soon as she got away from the pit, and she'd tried to call him right away, but he hadn't picked up.

She still woke up screaming from nightmares.

So did he.

Tim Harding's journal had not helped. Excerpts of it haunted his nights.

I shall always be indebted to the Author for putting me on this path. My daily diet of live spiders has already made a difference. After only three weeks, I am more vibrant and alive. I can feel myself growing more powerful each day. The venom treatments are also making me more resistant to the toxins of my arachnid friends...

I met the archaeologist, Dr. Michael Acres, today...

...Dr. Acres says that his work in Peru uncovered mystic knowledge regarding the Spider God...

...convinced me that there is a better means to using the Arachnida for even more power. They have invited me into their Circle and made me an initiate...

...Soon, I shall be the perfect servant, and I shall begin my transformation and become one of the Uttu-Ashipu, like the Acres before me...

With the help of the Internet, Ray learned that Uttu was a spider god from ancient Sumeria. An ashipu was, as far as he could make out, a conjurer of the gods.

The last sentence read:

Christine and Amanda shall help me achieve my life's purpose today. All gods require sacrifices, after all, and they will be the seminal gifts to the rebirth of a god! Uttu, Uttu! Come to us! Come to me! Grant me power beyond mortal imagining! Remake me in your image! Let me be one of the Apkallum!

Ray had let the fire at Spider Hill burn for over a week. It had consumed the Harding and Acres homes, as well as all the unoccupied houses and a good portion of the woods nearby. Once the fire burned itself out, one of the officers scouring the area spotted tire tracks traveling downhill toward the basement excavation where Ray had met Amanda Harding. They found Police Chief Ed Johansson's car submerged in the muddy water. His body sat in the car seat, buckled in, with hundreds of spider bites on his hands, arms, and face. Close to a dozen dead southern black widows were found in the car, presumably crushed by Ed as he struggled against some hell that Ray's imagination hounded him with in the waning hours of sanity. Ray had since learned that the "southern" black widow could be found as far north as Canada--and their venom was fifteen times more lethal than a rattlesnake's bite. That helped. Ray shuddered at the thought of Ed's body below the surface while he and Amanda chatted about reading and Tod Acres. Fingerprints on the trunk of the squad car indicated the car was most likely pushed into the excavated pit. The three sets of prints--two adults' and one child's--were not in the system.

The spider activity had died down somewhat over the past year, at least compared to that frenzied day in October, but remained inexplicably high for that area of Illinois. It also housed a disturbing variety of species that should not have been in the state, as well as several new species previously found no where else. When the county Corn Festival rolled around, people had been unwilling to use the Skip-2-Loo portable toilets because of the influx of spiders.

Ray had the house fumigated regularly now.

The feds had also been around, wanting to question the Acres for "irregularities in research importation procedures," but their car, and the Acres themselves, were never found.

Three days later, their postal worker, Larry Rosewall, delivered a package to the station addressed to Raymond Canfield, Braeburn Fire Chief. Inside was a wrapped box with a ribbon. Ray didn't think much of it, since people were often grateful to the firefighters for saving their homes or loved ones. He shook it gently, curious as to what it might be.

When he took the lid off the box, dozens of black widows ran out, and he got several bites on his hands. If it had not been for the antivenin they now kept on hand in the station and the rigs, he would have died within minutes. Fortunately for him, Maggie also kept a large can of spider spray in the dispatch office.

A card within read, "Best Wishes from the Acres." There was a picture of Tod Acres smiling into the camera. He was standing in front of a famous sculpture in Chicago called, "The Egg."

Last night, Ray and his crew had assisted with a fire in Springwater, the next town to the west. A house on the edge of a forest preserve caught fire from old wiring. Shortly after leaving the scene, Ray spotted an old abandoned farmhouse lit by a partial moon and the haze of starlight that still exists in the rural Midwest. A long, furrowed field of land, blue-gray in the eldritch night, led up to a decrepit barn sagging with age.

Next to the barn he spotted several people. Adults and children stood beside what he thought was an odd looking tractor or excavator. Maybe one of those foreign jobs. Even so, something about the shape of the tractor seemed wrong. Too curved in the back, too angular in the front.

When he took a second look, though, the tractor was gone. So were the people. All of them. Nowhere to be seen. Only then did he realize that they had been standing outside without any source of light, other than the moon.

He thought he saw a silhouette pass in front of the silvered light filtering through the barn's empty husk. Then he saw the people swarming up the sides of the barn and up onto the roof. Climbing. Like spiders.

His arms broke out in goose bumps, and he quickly looked away, some primordial, superstitious part of his being afraid that, if he kept looking, he would draw unwanted attention to himself. Ray's hand trembled when he lifted it from the steering wheel as he drove the rest of the way home. He couldn't sleep that night; the next morning, he and Brian drove back out there. The house and the barn were both abandoned, but showed signs of recent activity. Footprints, candy wrappers. No corpses, fortunately. And lots of spiders. Big, steering wheel sized spiders.

Ray took a long drag from his cigarette and flicked it out onto the runnels of gasoline he and Brian had laid down around the base of the house and barn. They watched for a while as the old, dry wood burned and tossed sparks into the early morning sky.

Weaver Of Dreams

By Anne Bishop

Anne Bishop is a New York Times bestselling author and the winner of multiple awards for the Novels of the Others, as well as the RT Book Reviews 2013 Career Achievement Award for her fantasy fiction, RT Book Reviews 2017 Career Achievement Award for her urban fantasy fiction, and the William L. Crawford Memorial Fantasy Award for the Black Jewels Trilogy. Her first novel, *Daughter of the Blood*, was published in 1998. Her most recent novel is *Lake Silence*, which she describes as a cozy thriller set in the world of the Others. She is currently working on *Wild Country*, another novel set in the Others' world. When she's not writing, Anne enjoys gardening, reading, and music. You can visit her at www.annebishop.com or keep up with news at annebishopscourtyard on Facebook.

1

Her web shook with the force of the storm. AboveWorld roared and flashed, turning dark-time to light-time. But there was something more, something different that trembled through the strand of silk. Something she'd never felt before.

AboveWorld roared and flashed again. Then something screamed — a terrible shuddering in her web — and a piece of AboveWorld crashed into World, ripping, tearing, roaring, shrieking.

Dark Wet splashed her, splashed her web, at the same moment something struck the web near the center. Prey?

Hunger overcame hesitation. She hurried along the threads, intending to secure her meal before heading back to the safer, more sheltered edge of her web.

But the something was hard and had no meat. As she tried to sink her fangs into it, she ingested some of the Dark Wet, and that...filled her, flowed through her, sang inside her.

Changed her.

After cleaning every bit of Dark Wet, she discarded the something and hurried back to the sheltered edge of her web to wait out the storm.

2

Light. And a hunger. For meat, yes. But also for something more.

Leaving her web, she traveled along the Rough that stretched out over World until she reached a place where the piece of AboveWorld had crashed into World. The Dark Wet still sang inside her, almost too quiet to feel, but it was enough to guide her to more of the Dark Wet.

Fixing an anchor thread to the Rough, she spun out silk. The World trembled with anger. The air quivered with grief and despair...and longing.

Her legs touched the piece of AboveWorld. Hard, like the something that had struck her web. Moving cautiously, she found a place where the Hard was torn away, revealing meat—and the Dark Wet.

After consuming as much of the Dark Wet as she could, she sank her fangs into meat and pumped her venom into the spot. It would only liquefy a tiny bit of meat, but that tiny bit would feed her well.

So she spun a web as close as she could to the meat—and the Dark Wet that seeped over the meat.

3

In dreams, she unfurled her wings and sailed through the Darkness—a vastness that was outside the body, and yet the body became its vessel; a power reached by heart and mind and spirit. Through it flowed the whispers of creation…and the silence of destruction. Her race had spiraled down its chasms and canyons and strange abysses for years beyond memory—and had understood that they would never understand this place that was, and wasn't, a place.

In dreams, the visions of webs shining in the Darkness hadn't dazzled and overwhelmed her mind, hadn't blinded her to the danger of the storm, and she had reached the caves on this island that she had chosen as her final resting place. But the wounds received because of the storm were fatal, and the caves were too far away.

No. Not quite true. She could have used her power to shift her broken body to the caves, but she felt a small tug, a small promise that her unique gift would not be lost if she remained where she was.

So in a dream that was more than a dream, she sent her last vision to her mother, Draca, showing her Queen how the new caretakers if the world would be able to travel safely through the Darkness: shimmering, colored webs of power that stretched through that vastness — pathways that could be reached from the Realms.

She could not say why the beautiful symmetry of the web resonated so strongly inside her, but the image didn't fade from her mind, despite the agony that clawed at her flesh. Nor could she say why, as she drifted between visions and dreams, she felt certain there was something nearby, something small and golden, that would be able to hold her particular gift.

She would have enough time. Just enough time. If this potential Weaver wanted what she had to give.

4

Light-time...day. Dark-time...night. AboveWorld...sky. Rough...tree. Hard...scale. Dark Wet...blood. Meat...

Sorrow. Pain. Longing. Need. Hope.

...dragon.

She...spider. Small. Golden.

Momentarily distracted by the strange thoughts, the spider returned to her housekeeping, rolled up the tattered remains of her old web, along with the discarded prey, then spun a fresh web. She did not spin in order to catch prey. She spun to keep other things away from the flesh that not only fed her body but sang to her about things she had never known existed. The World kept shifting as she absorbed the Weaver, showing her new things in the familiar.

Showing her ancient things in the familiar.

Showing her a Need for Weavers who could spin dreams into shapes that could walk in the World, for Weavers who could spin dreams into flesh.

She did not understand this Need, but it flavored the flesh her venom liquefied for her to ingest. So at night, when she was safely tucked beneath the scales in the hollow created by her feedings, she drifted on the tangled, silken threads of the dragon's longings and dreams—and began to learn how to weave a different kind of web.

5

Perhaps the other Seers were right. Perhaps her particular gift was too dangerous to give to the new caretakers of the Realms. Perhaps there was no other race that could, or should, take the deepest heart-dreams and provide a bridge for those dreams to become flesh.

But those dreams would be needed in the world. She knew that with unshakeable certainty. They would be needed—and it was unlikely even the simplest of those dreams would ever exist because she hadn't reached the caves as she'd intended. She wouldn't make the same transition as the rest of her race, transforming her scales into Jewels that would serve as a reservoir for the power the new caretakers could not contain in their smaller, weaker bodies. The Jewels that came from her should have been the vessels that contained her gift and would have changed the wearer into a Seer that could shape dreams into flesh. Now...

Did her mother know she was trapped on this island, exposed and dying? Did her sire, the great Prince of the Dragons, sense her fading presence in the world? Would they feel disappointment in her that, during moments of despair and heartache and hope, she was trying to pass her gift to a small, golden spider?

She should have stayed in the dark mountain that was the lair of the Prince and the Queen. She should have curled up in one of the deep hollows within that mountain and followed the rest of her race into the forever sleep. Instead she had followed a vision of a cave filled with dreams—a vision that would never come to pass.

Soon now. Soon. Her body was failing. Her power was fading. Soon she would be free of the world. Soon.

Closing her gold eyes, she drifted on dreams.

6

So much sorrow gave the flesh a bitter taste, but the spider remained, burrowing deeper beneath the scales for meat that still seeped blood, was still fresh. And it wasn't all bitter. When the daring male had approached her and indicated his willingness to mate, Dragon's flesh had been tastier that day, as if the mating had drawn sweeter memories to the surface.

Since she wanted her hatchlings to feed on this flesh that was making her more than just a spider, she worked to find a way to reach the memories, to see the dreams.

Dragon had shown her before. Why wouldn't Dragon show her now?

Frustrated, she climbed up to Dragon's jaw, anchored a strand of silk, and began to build a web. But as she built the web, she...felt things. So she spun them into the web, ignoring instinct and placing the threads where they needed to be. Sorrow. Pain. Longing. Need. Hope.

As she cautiously traveled the strands of the completed tangled web, warmth flowed through her. She paused, absorbed the feel of this sensations, and added one more small thread. Joy.

Suddenly she saw the caves, the place Dragon had intended to go to do the finest dreaming. And in those caves, she saw golden spiders, much larger than herself, spinning tangled webs.

Sound, faint and fading, filled her.

You have learned well, Dragon said. *But heed me, little one. You must guard the webs you weave that make dreams into flesh. Many beings will cherish those webs because they are spun out of magic that lives in the heart. But there will be others who will want to destroy that heart-magic before it can touch the world. Guard the webs...Weaver of Dreams*

Dragon's breath came out in a long sigh...and then there was silence.

7

The golden spider spun out the last thread of the web that filled the space between Dragon's jaw and shoulder. Most of her offspring had gone away, just ordinary spiders who would spin ordinary webs and catch ordinary prey. But the few who were different, who were like her, had stayed nearby, learning how to spin the tangled webs.

Despite the size of her web, she had caught only one small dream, but that one held a deep well of yearning...and a taste of sorrow that was, somehow, connected to Dragon. So she plucked the thread of yearning, sending it back to the heart it had come from.

As day turned to night, she settled into the most sheltered edge of her web—and wondered about the dreamer.

8

Day had barely touched the sky when she sensed a Presence that resonated with her tangled web. She waited, feeling the faint tremble of footfalls on the earth, the change in the air.

Sso. My daughter wass able to passs on her gift after all.

The voice that flowed through her felt like Dragon, but wasn't quite Dragon.

The Presence approached her web. Her offspring plucked the strands of their own webs, trying to ensnare the Presence's mind. But the Presence didn't respond, didn't give any sign that it had felt the tugs and whispers in those webs.

Blood sings to blood, the Presence said, leaning over the spider's tangled web. *Remember me.*

A drop of blood fell on a knot of tangled threads, a glistening bead of power.

The spider waited until the Presence went away before hurrying over to devour the offering.

Power flowed through her, a power even stronger and richer than Dragon's had been.

Draca.

Dragon's Mother. Dragon's Queen.

Remember me.

For hours that day, the spider stroked the strands of her tangled web, remembering Dragon, remembering the feel of Draca. Not shaped like Dragon, but still a dragon.

This dream web had done what it was meant to do. Draca would nor sorrow for Dragon anymore because she had seen that, in the most important way, Dragon was still in the world. Small now, and golden, but still in the world.

The spider carefully cut the anchoring threads and jut as carefully rolled the web into a cocoon. She traveled down Dragon's neck and shoulder until she reached the hole in the chest.

Perhaps it was the way of Dragon's kind, or perhaps it was some last bit of magic that had changed Dragon's flesh into porous rock covered with hard stone scales. Inside Dragon were several chambers where she could sin the first stage of a web, then listen, quiet and protected, while the strongest heart-dreams drifted over her, guiding her as she created her web.

The time would come when she and her offspring would make the long journey to the caves where the golden spiders would protect the webs of dreams that would become flesh. But not yet.

She squeezed through the opening that led to a small chamber and pulled the cocoon in with her.

Dragon's body was hollow stone now, but the heart hadn't rotted like the rest of the organs. It had changed to smooth stone. Whenever the spider came to this chamber and brushed a leg over that stone, the chamber filled with warmth, and she felt Dragon's joy that the Weaver's gift had not been lost.

The day would come when she no longer felt that warmth, and the stone would be no more than a stone. When that day came, she would leave. But even then, whatever bit of heart-memory might remain would be alone.

Before leaving the chamber, she spun out some silk and attached the cocoon of Draca's dream to Dragon's stone heart.

The Spider Under The Bed

By Chis Gerrib

Chris Gerrib admits to being a bit obsessed with Mars, but in a *healthy* way – all three books of his Pirate Series are set on Mars. Chris lives in the Chicago suburbs and still has a day job in IT. He holds degrees in history and business from the University of Illinois and Southern Illinois University. He also served in the US Navy during the First Gulf War, and can proudly report that not one Iraqi MiG bombed Jacksonville, Florida while he was in the service. In his copious free time, Chris is a past President of and currently active in his local Rotary club. His website is www.privatemarsrocket.net

"Mommy, there's a spider under my bed. Can you take care of her?"

Kim Garman regarded her daughter, barely four Standard years old, with a smile. "How did a spider get under your bed? Spiders live on Earth."

"This one doesn't."

Kim was positive that spiders were not on the approved list for this, the first colony on Two Charlie, the third moon of the second planet of the larger star in the Alpha Centauri system, but it was surprising the number of Earth-based creatures that had followed humans out into space. Spiders had gotten to Mars, and now a Martian spider had come with to Mars's first colony.

She grabbed a towel and followed her daughter down the narrow corridor of the prefabbed house to her bedroom. However the critter had gotten there, its days were over.

"She's under the bed, Mommy," her daughter said.

"Okay, Cassie," Kim replied. She got down on her hands and knees and, towel in hand, lifted up the bedsheet to look underneath. "Jesus Christ!" she

72

exclaimed, backpedaling furiously. That 'spider' was the size of a big damned dog!

"Mommy, bad word!" Cassie said.

Kim thought of several bad words as she dropped the towel and scooped up her daughter with one hand. The pair exited the room at speed and ran down to the only slightly larger master bedroom where Kim grabbed her Navy revolver.

"Stay here!" Kim said firmly to her daughter. Cocking the hammer of the gun, Kim returned to the other room.

The creature had emerged from the bed and was backed into a corner. It was the size of a big dog, a retriever or something.

"Mommy, she's hurt," Cassie said, running into the room and latching onto Kim's leg. Kim grabbed her daughter's hand to keep control of her. *I don't want to shoot it with her in here.* She looked at the monster again. *If that thing so much as blinks funny I'm emptying this gun into it, scared kid or not.*

"Mike!" Kim shouted, calling for her husband. "Get in here now!"

She was rewarded by the flushing of a toilet. "Coming!"

"Expedite!" Kim yelled as Cassie tugged at her hand.

Kim surveyed the creature. It had eight limbs, four on a side, but that was about the extent to which it resembled a spider. The leading-most set of limbs had apparently evolved into a set of manipulating limbs (arms?) and each ended with a trio of finger-like tentacles. The body was roughly tubular and unsegmented, and the eyes, on stalks, were vaguely mammalian. Given the number of weird animals they'd already seen on the moon, it was nothing too unusual. Except...

"What's so damned important?" Mike said, walking into the room. "And what's with the gun?"

Kim waved the gun at the spider. Mike's eyes followed. "Oh..." he started to turn white.

"If you faint on me, so help me..."

"I'm good," he said, moving to stand behind her. Not for the first time, Kim was wondering what she'd seen in him and why she thought he'd be able to handle a colonist's life.

"Take her," Kim said, gesturing with her chin at her daughter. "So I can take care of this."

"Mommy!" Cassie wailed. "She's hurt. Don't kill her!"

Kim looked at her daughter who was in tears. Mike didn't look too steady either. "Are the phones up?" Kim asked of Mike.

"Of course not."

They'd been on the planet a month and the low-tech cellular phone system had worked maybe two days altogether. She looked at the monster. If it wanted to hurt Cassie it already would have. She sighed heavily. "Go find Doctor McCloud and send somebody to City Hall. Move."

"Gone," Mike said, putting deed to word.

"She's hurt, Mommy," Cassie said again.

That didn't take a doctor to determine. The creature's left rearmost leg was hanging by a strip of skin and there were several other cuts in the body. It had got in a fight with something.

"That's why I asked for Doctor McCloud. He can help it."

"Not it, her. Her name is Daisy."

"You named her already?"

74

"No," Cassie said with only the asperity a four-year-old could generate. "That's her name. Well, as close as I can say it."

The creature made some noises. Kim heard an initial D and a trailing S, but the noise in-between was just that, noise. *Just how smart is this creature?* "How long has this..."

"Daisy,"

"Daisy been in your room? And is this the first time?"

"A little bit. I think she fell asleep under the bed. And this is the first time she's been on this side of the fence."

Or passed out, Kim thought. That green stuff looked like blood.

The fence Cassie was referring to encircled the small settlement, intended to keep critters out and kids in. Last week it had failed in the latter task, and Cassie had gotten lost in the forest outside of the fence. They'd found her just before dark in an area very close to the fence that had supposedly been searched twice. Kim blinked back tears from the memory. It had been the worst day of her life.

"Daisy helped me when I was on the other side of the fence," Cassie volunteered. "I told her she could come and visit me." To the creature, Cassie said, "I'm sorry you got hurt. Mommy will make it all better."

Daisy made some noises and bowed her eyestalks for a moment.

"This better be important," Doc McCloud said, walking in. "I was just getting ready to..."

"Important enough for you?" Kim asked.

"Where'd you find that?" McCloud asked.

"Under the bed. I was going to hit it with a towel."

McCloud saw Kim's gun. "I see you decided to upgrade."

"Seemed like a good idea." She looked at the gun in her hand. *I guess I'm not going to shoot it just yet.* Kim carefully lowered the hammer and stuffed the gun in her belt. Kim gestured at the, at Daisy. "She's hurt."

"She?"

"My daughter assures me she's a she and her name is Daisy. Can you help it?"

"I'm a doctor, not an entomologist," McCloud said.

"And if that's a bug, I'll eat my hat."

"I still have no idea how to treat it."

"Well, I'm just a Navy Lieutenant, but shouldn't that green stuff be on the inside?"

"Probably. Let's at least get the patient out where I can get to her," McCloud grumbled.

The damn thing made a sound that resembled 'thank you.'

A pair of sonic booms brought Kim out of a shallow sleep. She was laying on the narrow Government-issue recliner in their tiny living room. Daisy, bandaged as best as McCloud could, was laying on an exercise mat and had a blanket over her. Her eyestalks popped open at the boom, did a circuit, then lowered and closed. A bowl, glass and wooden spoon, the remains of a dinner of oatmeal and water, sat on the floor.

McCloud was on the couch, snoring softly. Cassie was curled up in a chair closest to Daisy. *So much for keeping a watch.* The door to the house opened and McCloud woke up as a Leading Astronaut from the comm-shack walked in.

"Lieutenant Garmin?" he asked. "Command wants you at the main hanger post-haste. Fleet's coming down."

"On my way," Kim said, clambering out of the chair. If they were flying a normal approach, she had fifteen minutes from the boom to get to the hanger, a three-minute walk. Plenty of time to take a leak.

Kim had even managed to score a cup of coffee (slightly-burnt, to be sure) in the hanger before the lander finished taxiing down the runway. It rolled to a stop in front of her, the tires squeaking on the metal grate over local grass analog that composed the airstrip. The lander's rear gate came down, and a group of five or six Navy techs with communication patches on their sleeves came hustling out. *Apparently comms are now a priority.*

The communication party was followed by a fire-team of Marines in battle gear. Finally Fleet Captain Erika Jansen, senior officer in the system, emerged, followed by a young female Lieutenant. Jansen marched right up to Kim, who saluted along with Colonel Singh, the colony commander. It didn't look like he'd gotten any sleep. Jansen, despite having to physically look up at Kim, had a way to make Kim feel small. Being very slow to return the salute was part of that way.

"Lieutenant Garmin," Jansen said. "First you lose a daughter, then you find a spider. What other surprises do you have in store for me?"

Jansen's still clearly pissed at me for Cassie's walkabout. I don't think she's the colonizing type.

"I don't know, ma'am, those were both surprises to me too."

"Surprises are for birthdays, Lieutenant, and it's not mine." Jansen glared at Colonel Singh. "Well?"

"Ma'am?" he said.

"This creature," Jansen said, irritation clear in her voice. "Native? Intelligent?"

"Possibly native, intelligence unknown," Singh replied.

"What?" Kim replied, earning a glare from both individuals. "I mean, the damn thing looks entirely different from everything we've found so far." Everything that they and the previous four expeditions had found had six appendages. Exothermic creatures had featherlike coverings, while endothermic creatures had large scales.

"So does an octopus," Singh said. "But the octopus definitely evolved on Earth." He sighed. "You're not suggesting it's non-native?"

Well, maybe I am. "But it's definitely intelligent," Kim said. "It named itself and demanded a spoon before it would eat."

"So it's one click up the scale from an octopus," Singh said.

"More than one click, sir. What about the spoon?"

"That is an interesting thing for an octopus to ask for," Jensen said. "I understand we found a backpack?"

"Yes ma'am, we did. Possibly of local manufacture."

"You should wonder, ma'am, how the creature asked for a spoon," Kim said.

"I did note that, Lieutenant," Jensen said, glaring at Kim. She looked as Singh. "Biochemical results?"

"Scientists are still working on it," Singh said. "It may have evolved from life ejected from Two." He was referring to the Neptune-sized gas giant that their moon, Charlie, was orbiting.

"Ma'am," Kim heard herself say, "My daughter is talking to it. This might be a spacefaring alien."

"When my kids were four they talked to everything," Jansen said. "And we've scoured this system looking for other ships."

"Did the things your kids talk to answer back, ma'am?" Kim asked.

"If you asked them, yes," Jensen said. To Singh, "Let's see the backpack."

We're doing all of this ass-backwards, Jansen thought as she followed the group to a side office in the hanger. Twelve years ago, Mars was being invaded by a coalition of Earth nations. The Republic of Mars Ship *Enki* and her sisters, blessed with viable force fields and anti-matter drive, had repulsed that invasion, and now the Martian Navy controlled the Solar system.

That same technology had allowed the development of a system to bend space and travel faster than light. Eight years ago, a Martian frigate, *RMS Tharsis*, made it to Alpha Centauri in only a year. But instead of using that technology to make peace with Earth, the politicians were relying on the Navy to hold off the Earthlings while Mars 'seized the high grounds' and colonized nearby star systems.

Jansen made a sour face. Earthlings understood basic physics too, and seeing that such ships were possible had led to massive investments in the science to build them. The prospect of getting locked into Earth's solar system had been merely an added spur to action. America and China had both gotten ships to the Centauri system, and supposedly a joint American-Japanese-Korean expedition was on the way. If this was a First Contact situation, or more accurately humanity's first First Contact situation, Jansen needed to have everything tied up before a potentially hostile task force arrived.

She followed Colonel Singh into a small office. "That's nylon," Jansen said, looking at a backpack laid out on a folding table. She touched a fitting. "And plastic." Other than a weird shape and complicated strapping system, it looked like the kind of load-bearing gear a human hiker would use.

"So where's the factory?" Jansen asked, examining some metal and plastic implements found in or near the pack. One of them looked like a pair of wire cutters. "No way this grew on a tree."

"Perhaps it was fashioned out of something we discarded," Singh offered.

"So you really have enough stuff down here that you can pitch it?" Jansen said. One of the expedition's supply ships, the *Wren Roberts*, had suffered a casualty in her FTL drive and was limping into the system. Spare *anything* was in short supply. "No, this came out of a factory."

"We haven't found any," Singh offered. "Perhaps a 3-D printer..."

"Which also doesn't grow on a tree," Jansen offered. "And how the hell do you get to 3-D printers without going through steam engines?" *It's starting to look a lot like this alien was from another star system. Which begs the question – where is their spaceship?* "Let's go see it."

Jansen walked into the Garmin's living room to see Len McCloud holding up a bedsheet. "Hi Erika," he said.

"What?" Jansen asked, gesturing at the bedsheet.

"She had to use the toilet," McCloud said. "Obviously wouldn't fit on ours, so we gave her a bucket. She wanted privacy."

A chirping noise came from the other side of the bedsheet. McCloud lowered it, revealing an eight-legged hairless dog lying on a pad. The two front legs were offering a plastic bucket with some sweet-smelling water in it. McCloud took the bucket and handed it to a rating, telling her to take it to the lab.

"This is the spider," Jansen said. She took a step towards it. One of her security people stuck out a beefy arm to stop her and she swatted it aside with irritation.

Jansen went to within a foot or so of the creature and took a knee, which put her nearly at eyestalk level for the standing creature. "What's your name?" Jansen said.

The creature made some noises, of which a leading D and a trailing S were intelligible. *Yep, Daisy or Desi, depending on your culture.* "Cassie, right?" Jansen said, looking at the human girl next to the creature.

"Yes ma'am," Cassie replied.

"Tell me how you know Daisy is a girl?"

"She told me."

"What exactly did she say?"

"It's a long story."

"We have time."

A four-year-old had her own sense of logic and story-telling, but the gist of it was that Cassie had gotten out of the fence and lost in the woods and Daisy had come across the girl. Cassie, lost and scared, had screamed, and Daisy scurried away.

Daisy then returned and was eventually able to lead the girl to the fence area. On the way, the creature had stopped to urinate and Cassie, not seeing "boy parts" decided Daisy was a girl. "Do you know why Daisy went away?" Jansen asked.

"No," Cassie replied.

"Is it possible Daisy had friends in the woods?" Jansen asked.

"I guess so," Cassie answered.

"Well, don't you think we need to get Daisy back with her friends?"

"Probably. But she just got here."

"Remember when you were lost?" Jansen said. "And how your mother acted when you got back?"

"Yes,"

"Well, Daisy's friends are thinking the same thing."

Cassie looked dubiously at Daisy. "She can't walk."

"We'll take her," Jansen said. She looked at the group and stood up. "Get a wheelbarrow and an operator. We're going on a hike."

"Fleet Captain Jansen," her Flag Lieutenant said. "Per regulations..."

Jansen glared at her aide. "I've been cooped up on that," she looked down at little Cassie and swallowed the Navy language that was bubbling out, "ship for months. I'll be hanged if I miss out on this because of regulations. Now, unless you want to be busted to Astronaut Recruit, get me a wheelbarrow or the local equivalent and let's move while we've still got light."

An hour later, a party stepped out of the fence at the gate nearest where the creature had cut a hole in and headed off. The party consisted of Lieutenant Garmin, with a slung shotgun, her daughter with pink backpack, two Marines from Jansen's protective detail paired with a duo of scouts from the colony, all four with rifles, a sturdy-looking fellow operating the two-wheeled cart, and McCloud. The group was larger and more heavily-armed then Jansen had wanted, but she'd gotten tired of people quoting regulations at her.

The moon didn't have a magnetic field worth noting and the gas giant's field made compasses dizzy, so they relied on storms on the face of the gas giant for directions. For this to work, one needed to know what time it was, so Jansen could see how easy it was to get lost.

They headed in what Jansen was told was an easterly direction. After a good hour, they hit what the colonists were calling Lake Mariner. Jansen thought it was more like a pond with delusions of grandeur, but it was the second-biggest surface water feature within a day's walk of the colony. Not for the first time, Jansen wondered whose bright idea it was to base the colony in the middle of a flat semi-wooded plain.

"Rifles out," one of the scouts, Ferguson, said. "P-crocs."

P-crocs or pseudo-crocodiles were what they were calling an endothermic animal that occupied the same spot in the food chain as crocodiles back on Earth. They tended to bite first and worry about indigestion later. Jansen unholstered her revolver, thinking she should have taken a long-barreled version instead of the snub-nose she was carrying.

Daisy made a complicated set of noises and a circular motion with a tentacle. "I guess we're going around the lake," Jansen said. It did not take a biologist to tell that the creature was fading fast. *I'd hate to return a body.*

A few hundred meters on, they stopped while Cassie rejoiced in the finding of her doll. No wonder they didn't find her, Jensen thought. This is quite a ways out from the colony.

They had just resumed moving when Ferguson, on point, called a halt. "Something in the woods, one o'clock," he said quietly.

"P-crocs?" Jansen asked.

"Not unless they sprouted more legs," he replied.

"Cassie," Jansen said, "ask Daisy to say hi."

To Jansen's surprise, Cassie made some noises, mostly hoots with a few whistles and clicks. "What did you just tell them?"

"Daisy told me to say that."

"Okay," Jansen said, blinking a drop of sweat out of her eye, "I guessed that. What does it mean?"

"I think it means I'm hurt, help me," Cassie said. "That's what she said last night."

And a little child shall guide us, Jansen thought, suppressing hysterical laughter.

"They're coming," Ferguson said as bushes in front of him started to rustle.

"Nobody shoot, repeat do not shoot," Jansen said in a low voice. "In fact, sling rifles." She holstered her pistol as her troop slowly slung their weapons.

The bushes parted to reveal four spiders. There was maybe 10% spread in size between the spiders, with backpacks on, and Daisy. Three of the spiders were carrying what looked to be projectile weapons. As the humans slung their weapons, the spiders put theirs in long leather-ish bags on their back.

"Wheelbarrow front," Jansen said. The wheelbarrow man rolled forward, stopping when he was even with Jansen. "Take her on in," Jansen said. "Leave the wheelbarrow."

After a long pause, he did as directed. Once the wheelbarrow was with the spiders, one of the spiders, the one not obviously armed, started examining Daisy. The arms move fluidly, almost bonelessly. What looked like a hypodermic needle was produced from the backpack and used to inject Daisy.

"Will she be alright?" Cassie asked.

The medical spider looked up and said something, then resumed working.

84

"Well?" Jansen asked.

"Yes, I think," Cassie replied.

"Now what, Captain?" Ferguson asked.

"Now we leave," Jansen replied. "Nice and easy." She turned and started to walk away, but a loud whistle stopped her. She turned around to see one of the spiders scrambling towards them. It caught up to the group and clearly waved at the other spiders.

"Boss?" Ferguson asked.

"Looks like Cassie's got a new friend," Jansen replied. "Cassie? Do you think you can tell them we'll be back here in a week?"

"How many days is a week?"

She is four, for Pete's sake. "Do you know the word for day?"

"Yes." Cassie made a sound.

"Say it again." As she did, Jansen held up five fingers, deciding on the fly to keep it simple. Jansen then tapped her chest and pointed to the ground. "One more time please," Jansen asked while repeating the show.

"Big one says yes," Cassie translated. She looked at the smaller spider. "I'm Cassie," she said, tapping her chest. "What's your name?"

The new spider made noise, an R and V prominent. "Rover," Cassie pronounced.

"Rover it is," Jansen said. She looked at the others. "Home, please." *That went quite well.*

"This rifle's weird, ma'am," Garmin said. They were at her house while her husband was cooking dinner. It smelled a lot better than shipboard food, although how much of that was just because it was by a different cook Jansen couldn't tell. Cassie and Rover were playing catch in the front yard with a soccer ball. *Perhaps I was a bit too harsh on Garmin when her kid got lost.*

"Weird how?" Jansen asked.

"Well, it's a black powder round with a hard lead ball and an exposed hammer, but there's a transfer bar."

Jansen knew the minimum required by the Navy to carry a gun, and that minimum did not include transfer bars. She said as much.

"A transfer bar is a piece of metal between the hammer and the firing pin. It prevents a sharp blow on the hammer firing the weapon."

"Sounds like a good idea. So?"

"So, weapons in our black powder era didn't have that. Modern replicas did. But more importantly, why a nylon backpack and a black powder gun?"

"Good question."

Thirty-five days, Jansen thought, staring at the tactical display in her flag plot. Thirty-five days since she'd hiked across the plain to exchange Daisy for Rover. Their pair of linguists had been hard at it, but a lot of questions were still unanswered.

"Where do you come from?" had produced a noun, but not a useful one. "Why are you here?" had resulted in "to become older" which wasn't very helpful. And things they thought they knew were wrong as well. The spiders weren't 'boy' and 'girl' – they each could both lay and fertilize eggs.

The Americans were coming, along with their Japanese and Korean allies. Three ships from Earth, ships that would be in orbit by the end of the day. And once they were in orbit, Jansen would have to disclose the existence of the spiders.

Technically, Jansen did not need to reveal the aliens existence to the combined force heading her way. Very technically, Jansen could claim the entire moon as a 'scientific and research' station and deny the multinational force landing rights. She even had more firepower than the multinationals did – she had three frigates plus support ships while the force approaching her was only three lightly-armed exploratory ships.

As a practical matter, denying landing rights would start a war, something well above Jansen's paygrade. If they landed, it was highly unlikely that the Martians had stumbled across the only group of spiders on the planet. Time was not on her side. At least the *Roberts* had finally got in, which meant that the noisy fan in her flag plot had been replaced.

"Captain," her Chief Astronaut said. "Ground needs you on secure six."

She put on her headset and dialed up the frequency. "Jansen, over."

"It's Garmin, ma'am. Rover's going apeshit down here, saying 'it's time,' over."

Bad word, Lieutenant, Jansen thought, reminded of Garmin's daughter Cassie. "Copy. Time for what, over?"

"No idea," Garmin replied. "Anything unusual going on upstairs, over?"

"Negative. Force approaching is coming straight down the middle – wait one, over." A new contact appeared on her screen. Too close and too large. She keyed to fleet broadcast and went out in the clear. "All units, break and evade, repeat break and evade, over!"

She felt her ship lurch underneath her as it suddenly changed course to avoid colliding with the asteroid-sized object that had appeared in orbit ahead of them. She scrambled to buckle up in her seat as the ship maneuvered again. Other ships in the formation also made sudden moves to avoid a collision.

"Get me a visual!" Jansen barked. One of the watchstanders pulled up a camera feed and dumped it on the main screen. It didn't look large, until Jansen realized it was an unmagnified feed of a ball two kilometers in diameter. The operator magnified the feed, revealing a featureless plain.

"Looks like a forcefield," the Chief of the Watch said.

Jansen toggled back to secure six. "A ship the size of an asteroid just dropped into orbit," she said over the link.

"Rover just disappeared!" Garmin said.

"You let him get away?"

"No, ma'am, I was watching him and he just disappeared."

"You'd better check the video, out," Jansen said. She turned her attention to her fleet, which was busily dodging the object – an object that just hung in space stationary over the moon. It was not in orbit, nor was it falling or accelerating out. It just hung, somehow generating and expending an incredible amount of energy to hover.

"The Americans on international five," the Chief of the Watch said. "Five second speed-of-light delay," she added helpfully.

"Copy." Jansen went out over international five, one of the radio frequencies set up for safety in space. "Multinational task force, this is Martian Navy Task Group Two-two, over."

Ten seconds later, five out and five back, came the reply. "Group two-two, this is Group Unity. We see a large space station trailing your formation. What is that, over?"

"Unity, this is two-two. That's no station, that's a spaceship. Non-human, repeat non-human ship, over."

After another irritating delay, the Americans came back with "please don't lie to us, over."

"Look at your damn data logs, you idiot," Jansen sent back. "It just popped into being. We've encountered non-human intelligence on the planet. These non-humans are not, repeat not, native to this system. I don't know how or if this ship is related to that, over." The spider was definitely out of the bag.

By the time Jansen's ships completed an orbit, the alien ship had obligingly moved to a higher latitude on the moon, allowing Jensen's ships to pass by without incident. Garmin and Singh, on the moon, had reviewed the video logs and Rover had just vanished between frames.

On the second orbit, the alien ship started broadcasting on international five. It first came out with a lengthy blast in Spider, then followed up with English.

"This is ship of what you call Spiders," the broadcast began. "It is good name for us. We thank you for care shown to one of us you call Daisy, and wish your youth Cassie many eggs."

"This ship bring home our youth, who on this moon gain primitive survival learning. You are okay to stay. We return six travels this moon about planet with smart spiders to learn of humans. Message repeats twice."

After the third repetition, the ship quietly winked out of existence. Jansen stared at the speaker and the now-blank screen where the ship had been. "It's a damn Boys and Girls Scout camp," she said.

"They'll be back in forty-two days," the Chief of the Watch said.

Spinster

By Lauren Lyn Cidell

Lauren Lyn Cidell "began making up stories as soon as she could talk", according to her parents. Two cats let her live with them in the suburbs of Chicago. An avid fan of history and SF, she is a proud member of the League of Intrepid Travelers and Explorers.

Vessa breathed through her mouth in an effort to quell her urge to gag. Had it only been the blood stench of freshly killed and skinned carcasses (rabbits mostly with a few goats and the odd haunch of cattle) she could've borne it better. No, it wasn't the dead creatures that bothered her but the living.

Below them in three uniform rows, five dozen spinsters dozed in front of their looms. Human workers in heavy canvas armor used *ferrigent* blades to cut the webs of bloodsilk from each loom. In another part of the mill those webs would be processed into thread and ultimately cloth.

Impervious to wind, fire and water, bloodsilk, so named for its vivid red color, fetched high prices in every market in the known world. It could only be cut by implements made of *ferrigent*, the sacred alloy of steel and silver. Over time though the red color would darken to black at which point the fibers would disintegrate into dust.

The clatter of metal falling on stone drew her attention back the floor below. One of the workers had dropped a knife.

Nobody moved. One of the creatures opened an eye, a solid black eye darker than the deepest cavern.

Just when Vessa thought the air would burst her lungs, the spinster closed its eye and resettled itself in its nest. All seemingly well again the other workers went about their business.

Vessa glanced over at Daenyl to see his reaction. He appeared more fascinated than horrified. Her centurion had warned her that when Sorcerers' talents manifested, they often lost most if not all of their sense of self-preservation. From what Vessa had seen so far, Daenyl was no exception.

Once general schooling was finished, all Sorcerers were required to spend a year of their lives traveling before entering an apprenticeship. It had been Vessa's bad luck to be chosen as Daenyl Macawen's companion for his journey. As the best fighter in her class she'd expected a serious posting, along the Border perhaps. Instead she'd been stuck riding herd on some wizardling who'd had to be dragged from the Laboratorum honking and howling the whole way. And not just any wizardling but one she'd loathed on sight, and who returned the sentiment.

The day before her thirteenth birthday on a visit to the market Vessa had slipped the leash of her governess and run up to a troop of Agate Legionnaires and begged to draw one of their swords. A Legionnaire's consecrated sword could only be drawn by one deemed worthy to wield it.

The troop leader had unslung his longsword from his back and proffered it to her. Vessa had grasped the hilt with both hands and pulled with all her might.

The sword came free so easily that its weight overbalanced her. She had landed on her backside in a puddle, much to the amusement of the boy being escorted to Redstaff Castle to begin training to develop his talents for Sorcery. He'd laughed so hard he'd nearly tumbled off his pony.

Twelve years later she and that same boy had ridden into Cheverport, the first stop on their journey. They'd taken rooms at the inn and then went to report to the resident Sorceress. They'd arrived at the same time as the courier from Jeorge Araignier, owner of the bloodsilk mill requesting assistance. Daenyl and Vessa had been dispatched forthwith.

"What do you know about spinsters?" Araignier asked as he, Daenyl and Vessa sat down to tea in his private parlor.

"The first spinster was created by Maltalius," Daenyl replied. "He transformed a human woman using a concoction of blood, venom, and silk from a macrantula."

From the corner of his eye Daenyl had seen Vessa cringe at his reference to the giant cave-dwelling spiders of Kafria. Not that he held that against her. Macrantulas laid eggs the size of watermelons and grew to the size of ponies. He certainly had no wish to find himself face to face with one.

"Spinsters secrete bloodsilk from their bodies," Daenyl continued. "They sleep during the brightest hours of the day and will only eat raw meat. Supposedly a drop of their venom will transform a human woman into a spinster as well."

Daenyl was more inclined to think that last part was a story made up by some boy to terrify his sister. There were no credible accounts of such things ever happening.

"Average lifespan is between a dozen and two dozen years," he went on. "Instead of decomposing, the body secretes a resin that essentially turns the skin into a husk. In about six weeks that husk will crack open like a hatching egg to reveal two to three daughters."

"And when that happens we keep them isolated until they reach maturity," Araignier said pouring himself more tea. "We use that time to get them accustomed to the routine of sleep, eat, spin."

Daenyl nodded. The creatures he'd seen had appeared placid enough. Of course they might be very different when they fed.

"When number 10642 died, we moved her body into the hatching room. She was rather large, much bigger than any of the others, but since she displayed no aggression I thought nothing of it. When the morning shift started they found three infant spinsters and evidence of a fourth. And the attendant on duty the night before has since disappeared."

"You suspect him of taking the fourth, creature?" Vessa asked.

"He certainly had means and opportunity," Araignier replied. "And as to motive, last fall a Scienturgist came here offering five thousand ducats for my next dead spinster."

Daenyl felt his jaw clench at the name. The Scienturgists claimed that all Sorcerers were no more than tricksters and charlatans preying on the gullible and ignorant. Anyone, they said, could learn the Sacred Wisdom regardless of whether they had some alleged blood-gift.

Of course the Scienturgists went on to claim that the Sacred Wisdom wasn't sacred at all. That concepts such as blessedness and cursedness were mere chicanery intended to dupe the unsophisticated into believing that Sorcery was some unfathomable power that only a privileged few could use.

For now the so-called College of Scienturgy amounted to little more than malcontents, but they were gaining popularity and prestige.

"I refused of course," the miller continued, "but he insisted the offer was still open. I was able to bar him from the premises, but I couldn't exactly prevent him from approaching my workers in the village."

Five thousand ducats was more money than most folks saved in a lifetime. Even if the Scienturgists only paid a tenth of that for the creature, it was still a considerable amount.

"Did he have a sweetheart?" Vessa asked.

"I couldn't say," Araignier said his tone conveying confusion at the relevance of the question.

"Do you happen to have any fragments of the original husk?" Daenyl asked. "If so I can use it focus a tracking crystal."

"As a matter of fact I do," the miller said standing up. At the door he hesitated. "If it's possible, please bring her back alive," he said. "It's not her fault she is what she is."

All swaddled up like this she didn't look any different from a human infant, Coty thought as he trekked along the river. At least, until she yawned revealing tiny conical teeth.

He'd already learned the hard way that she wouldn't eat fish. He'd been lucky in finding a trapper willing to trade a brace of rabbits for 3 fine trout.

There'd been a tense moment when the man's wife had asked to hold the baby. Coty had declined on the grounds that his daughter's health was still fragile despite surviving the fever which had killed her mother.

Coty reached into his pocket for another *kaufi* bean and popped it into his mouth. He needed to be awake and on the move, at least until he got to the city of Spira.

Once he received payment, he would treat himself to a room at one of the finer inns.

Spurred by the stimulants of the *kaufi* and visions of a night of indulgence he walked on.

"Know your quarry," the hunter-witch who'd taught tracking at Redstaff instilled into Vessa. She wanted to learn as much about Coty as she could. He was a recent hire at the mill and his overseer had only described him as a good worker.

"How long will it take you to focus that tracking crystal?" she asked as they neared the inn.

"As long as it takes," Daenyl replied with that note of condescension in his voice that made her want to throttle him.

"Well, while you're doing that, I'd like to make some inquiries."

"Go," he said with a flippant wave of his hand like he was shooing away an annoying insect. He headed inside. Hopefully he could work his bit of alchemy without blasting himself or anybody else to smithereens. Not that Daenyl's demise would upset her, she just didn't want to have to deal with the paperwork.

Know your quarry. Well, Coty was in his twentieth year and lodged at Madame Stadhurst's boarding-house at the west end of the village. Vessa opted to walk and left her horse in the care of the inn's ostler.

SPINSTER

●●●

Back at the inn Daenyl shut himself in his room. He placed his Satchel on the table. He carefully detached one of the patches to reveal square gems in thirteen different colors each about the size of a raspberry. He picked up the blue one and set it into the indentation of the Satchel's clasp. He waited three seconds and then opened the Satchel and took out his Codex. He shut the Satchel, waited another three seconds and then removed the blue gem. He then repeated the process with the red gem this time removing a blank tracking crystal, his crucible with its stand and a stoppered flask of blessed water.

Sorceresses and even many Sorcerers opted to store their spellgems in the form of jewelry. As a former pickpocket Daenyl preferred to hide his altogether.

The husk fragments the miller had provided had crumbled to dust. Well, at least it saved him the bother of having to grind them up. Opening his Codex to the appropriate page he went through the ritual to focus the tracking crystal on the spinster.

Once it was complete he used a pair of tongs to remove the crystal from the crucible and set it into a pewter lattice. Taking the attached chain he held it up to examine it.

The core color was the same vivid red as bloodsilk but it was mottled by splotches of gray and brown. It reminded him of a redlight that hadn't been cleaned in an age.

Well, it didn't have to be pretty, it just had to work. He spoke the incantation to activate it and turned slowly in a circle.

The core red color glowed brighter and brighter and he could feel the vibrations as he faced northwest. In the exact direction of the bloodsilk mill.

Daenyl sighed and struck his forehead with the heel of his hand. He should've realized. After all the missing spinster's three clutchmates were back at the mill and their close proximity only amplified the signal.

If only he'd thought to obtain blood samples from the others he could have configured the crystal to ignore them.

He unwound the chain and set to work cleansing and putting away his tools. Vessa would be back at any moment.

The brisk *tap-tap* on the door signaled her return. He went and opened the door.

Most female Legionnaires wore their hair in a simple braid, but Vessa kept hers cropped short. The style suited her, he decided. She looked like a wood faerae, one of the fabled Champions of the Forest.

"So did you find out if Coty had a sweetheart?" Daenyl asked standing back to let her enter.

"In a sense," Vessa said as she walked in, her eyes instinctively scanning the room.

"It seems Coty fancied himself in love with the mayor's daughter."

"And that means what?" Daenyl asked as he closed the door.

"It speaks to his motive," Vessa said squaring off to face him. "From what I gather Coty was more careful with his money than most young men his age. He had nearly 300 ducats in the local depository, none of which he withdrew. Why would he leave his life savings behind unless he planned to come back?"

A valid point, Daenyl thought.

"I've also determined that Coty did not own a boat or a horse. Nobody remembers him booking passage on a ferry or a coach and none of the livery stables rented him a horse."

"So we can safely assume he's traveling on foot overland," Daenyl said.

"If he hopes to sell the spinster to the Scienturgists, he'll head for Spira."

Daenyl agreed. The College of Scienturgy was part of Spira's famous Polygnostic University. "How long would it take him to get there?"

"That depends on his route. My guess is he'll stay within sight of the river to avoid getting lost. He's not used to walking though and carrying that creature will slow him down. I've asked Captain Desmet for some fresh mounts. I believe we can pick up his trail soon. That is, with your permission, Wise One,"

Daenyl tensed. The mode of address was entirely proper, but something in the way she said it suggested contempt rather than respect.

Daenyl had been born in the brothel where his mother had found refuge after her sanctimonious parents kicked her out of their home. She'd worked as a laundress, not a whore, but that distinction had not mattered to the more nobly born students at Redstaff.

And they didn't come much more nobly born than Vessa. The Lady Vessandra was the third child and only daughter of the Duke of Luziana.

He smiled to himself remembering the sight of Lady Vessandra on her backside, mud all over her pink silk gown. Seeing one of the high-and-mighties down in the muck had thrilled him that day.

"By all means," he replied with the cold courtesy he'd perfected by his second year of study.

"Nobody at his lodgings saw him after he went to work the night of the hatching," Vessa remarked as they mounted their borrowed horses. "I'm betting that he followed the mill's canal to the river and went north."

Once they reached the mouth of the mill's canal it didn't take her long to spot his tracks. "He can't be too far ahead of us," she said moving her horse along the trail. "What I'm wondering is how he plans to contain it."

"It, oh, you mean her."

Vessa stopped her eyes mid-roll. Daenyl's persistence in anthropomorphizing the creature worried her. He may have been lulled by the placidity of the creatures at the mill, but Vessa had kept a hand on her sword until there was a locked oakstone door between them and those abominations.

It wasn't that she despised them so much as she feared them and she wasn't ashamed to admit it. Macrantulas were of the Creator's own making and thus served some purpose in the Grand Design. But spinsters were spawned of dark magick. As far as Vessa was concerned the benefits of bloodsilk did not balance the risks of keeping such creatures as livestock.

"These creatures are nocturnal," Vessa pointed out. "So either he sleeps when it does or he has to have some way of keeping it from wandering off in the night, or worse, attacking him."

Much as he wanted to Daenyl couldn't deny that Vessa had logic on her side. Coty couldn't hope to walk to Spira in a single day. He would need to rest at some point.

They rode for about an hour when a scent caught Vessa's attention.

"What is it?" Daenyl asked.

"Pan fried trout, unless I miss my guess."

They followed the aroma to a cabin deeper in the woods. If the various skins stretched out to dry were any indication it was home to a trapper and his family. As they rode into the yard a man came to the doorway.

"Hello," Vessa said before Daenyl could open his mouth. "We're looking for a friend of ours who may have passed through recently." She gave him the description provided by Coty's landlady.

"Yeah," the trapper said turning his head and spitting a gumnut onto the ground. "Fella like that came through this afternoon. Traded his trout for some rabbits. We offered to put him up for the night, but he was determined to keep on going. You should be able to catch him easy. Can't imagine he'd get too far with his daughter."

"His daughter?" Daenyl asked.

"Yeah, he kept her all swaddled up. Mother died of a fever."

"Well, thank you for your help," Vessa said.

Coty lay on his belly scooping water from the river to drink. Along this part of the shore the waterline was just low enough that if he tried to do it while kneeling, he'd be certain to fall in.

Face it, he told himself, you're not going to reach Spira before dark. There were some caves nearby. He'd rest there and get a fresh start in the morning.

An unexpected roar from behind had him scrambling to turn over. Before getting his drink he'd tucked the spinster into a tree. He turned just in time to see her rip open the neck of a small bear collapsed against that same tree.

Coty froze. At the mill the spinsters were fed using a system of large buckets and pulleys. Nobody *ever* went down on the mill floor while they were eating. He'd have to wait until she finished before he could move on again.

"What is that?" Daenyl asked.

Vessa picked up what looked to be an old wet rug and held it out at arm's length. "Best guess, I'd say a woodland she-bear," she said as she examined the hide. "Old enough not to need her mama but not old enough to be a mama."

She lowered her arms and surveyed the ground. "She probably surprised Thief while he was fishing and then the spinster surprised her."

Daenyl looked away from the pile of bones and viscera before his gorge rose any further. "How big do you think she is now?"

"You tell me," Vessa said wiping her hands on some leaves and remounting her horse. "As I understand it the more it eats the faster it grows. I doubt it's still small enough to pass for a human child. The question is, what will Coty do when he realizes that?"

Coty leaned against the wall of the cave pondering the fragments of all his hopes and dreams. His plan, which had seemed so clever at the time, had come to nothing. His arms ached and his feet burned from the unaccustomed hike.

Right now the spinster was happily spinning her first web. She was about the size of a goat now. Even if he could swaddle her up, she was too heavy to carry.

But, maybe, what if, what if he just left her here? Could he?

His thoughts jerked to a stop as he felt the prickle of a spider crawl across his skin. He instinctively flicked it off and crushed it beneath his heel.

The last sound he heard was the horrific screech of the spinster's outrage as she sank her mandibles and fangs into his throat.

"Well," Vessa said as she poked through the remains with the tip of her shortsword, "now we have no choice. We have to kill it."

"Do we?" Daenyl asked.

Vessa settled into fighting stance as she stood. "You cannot possibly be serious."

He wouldn't look at her.

"This isn't some stray lamb or calf that we've been tracking," she said. "It has tasted human blood, Daenyl. You know the law as well as I do."

"Yes, I know damn it!" Daenyl burst out. "I just wish there was another way than simply killing her."

"Believe it or not, I do too."

Now he turned to face her, disbelief plain on his face.

Vessa sighed. "I don't relish violence," she said speaking so softly he had to step closer to hear.

"I didn't grasp that sword that day in the market because I wanted to. I did it because ever since I first learned who the Legionnaires are and what they do, what we do, I knew that was the path I was destined to take. Every time I mentioned it my mother slapped me down. Whenever any Legionnaires came to the palace she actually locked me in my apartments under guard."

She paused to brush some moisture from her eyes.

"I knew that after that day I would never get another chance, that I would spend the rest of my life under a cloud of regret if I failed to become what the Creator clearly meant me to be. So when the opportunity came I grabbed at it with both hands."

"And landed on your ass in the mud," he quipped.

She laughed, as he'd hoped.

"Sometimes I think Mother was more upset that I'd ruined my dress than that I'd drawn the sword."

She was so pretty when she smiled.

"So. Do you think we're far enough away from the mill for that tracking crystal of yours to work?"

"How did you-" He stopped speaking as she raised an eyebrow at him and reached into his pocket and pulled out the crystal on its chain. It led them deeper into the cave.

Vessa went back to secure the horses and extracted a glowgem from her saddlebag. Returning to the cave she said the coin-sized disc into a headband. The stone projected a beam of light about fifty paces ahead of her. As she secured it around her head she noted that Daenyl had set three pea-sized glowgems into the frames of his Spectacles. They made him look older somehow, more scholarly.

Vessa drew both her swords and gestured for Daenyl to get behind her as they headed deeper into the cave.

Daenyl had never been afraid of the dark in general. The part of Nolliens he'd lived in for the first twelve years of his life didn't really come alive until nightfall.

When the Dean had talked to him about his journey the older man had told him that no, Daenyl would not be allowed to spend half a year at sea and then the other half coming home. The point of the journey was for Sorcerers to be among the people, serving as needed.

Daenyl had resigned himself to a route that would take him criss-cross over the continent with appointed stops where he would be at the disposal of the resident

Sorcerer. It was Vessa's task to keep him alive and aid him to the best of her abilities.

At the start of this journey he hadn't thought she would be of much use. Now he was very glad and very grateful that Vessa and her swords were between him and a feral spinster.

The crystal pulsed bright red. That was the only warning he had before she dropped down from the darkness above them hissing and snarling.

Daenyl jerked back and tripped over a rock. He came down on his backside hard enough to knock his Spectacles from his face.

In the light from her headband he saw Vessa stab the creature in the torso. She had been aiming for where the heart would be in a human.

But spinsters weren't human.

Vessa realized her mistake as the creature turned on her. The only way she could be sure to kill it would be to slice its head off, but she had to get it down first.

Daenyl had just put his Spectacles back on when he heard a sickening wet *swish* followed by a *thunk*. Looking up he saw Vessa standing, breathing hard, blood dripping from both her swords.

The spinster lay on the ground. Her severed head lay facing so that it seemed she was looking at her own dead body.

"Now what?" Vessa asked. "I don't know about you, but I have no intention of dragging this," and she paused to kick the carcass in the abdomen wincing as a remnant of bloodsilk oozed out, "all the way back to the mill."

"I'll handle it," he told her.

While Vessa cleaned her weapons, Daenyl took six crystalsheets from his Satchel and using a bit of levitation managed to encase the remains. Once the seams were fused he used a resizing charm to make it fit into a common oakstone lockbox. After that he secured it in his Satchel using the black gem.

He looked over at Vessa and saw the holes in her bracer where the spinster had sunk its fangs.

"Are you hurt?"

Vessa unbuckled it. There were two red marks on her arm but the skin wasn't pierced. "I should be all right."

Daenyl was in no mood to take chances on should-be's. He led Vessa back out of the cave and used a whole vial of blessed saltwater to cleanse her arm. And then for good measure he wrapped it with aloe leaves and linen.

"We'll have Junitta look at it when we get back to Cheverport," he said naming the town's resident Sorceress.

"I'm touched by your concern," Vessa said with considerably less sarcasm than usual.

"Well," Daenyl said trying to sound gruff, "if you die the Creator only knows what kind of lunkhead I'd be stuck with. At least you're housebroken."

She really did have a nice laugh, he thought as he secured his Satchel to the saddle.

Chosen

(Excerpt from AGE OF ANANSI)

By James Lovegrove

James Lovegrove has written over 50 acclaimed novels and children's books. His most recent works include the Pantheon series of which the following story is part. Learn more about him at www.jameslovegrove.com

Everything would have been fine, it it wasn't for the spider.

The spider came along , took a perfect life, a life that was well planned and blameless—*my* life—and wrecked it.

Maybe I should begin this the way my grandmother taught me to, by reciting the traditional incantation: "We do not really mean, we do not really mean that what we are about to say is true. A story, a story. Let it come, let it go."

Nanabaa Oboshie smelled of spices and fat-lady sweat. I'd cuddle up on her capacious lap and she would tell me the old Ashanti myths. Her English wasn't good, thickly accented, but I loved the cadences of her speech, the singsong rhythms, the occassional incomprehensible lapses into Kwa phraseology.

Most of the stories, the best ones, were about Anansi.

Anansi is lord of stories. He won ownership of them off his father Nyame, the Sky God. He bought them by trapping Onini the Python, Osebo the Leopard, the Mmoboro Hornets and Moatia the Dwarf, and handing these prizes to Nyame. Through stealth and subterfuge he captured the creatures, and so all the world's stories became Anansesem — Anansi stories.

Which is, of course, a story in itself.

"We do not mean that what we are about to say is true.

Only it *is* true.

It happened to me.

My name is Dion Yeboah, and up until not long ago I was a respectable and respcted barrister, specialising in criminal law. I had a sterling reputation as a defence QC, the man you want on your side when you're in a jam, the man whose silver tongue and sharp legal brain could scoop you out of hot water andland you safely on the right side of the bars of a prison cell.

I charged the going rate for my servics, which is to say 'a lot,' and I can't confess to ever feeling guilty about that. And yes, there may have been a time or two when I acted as counsel for a client whose innocence I wasn't entirely convinced of. But everyone is entitled to a fair trial, and that means a robust defence. Besides, I did my share of *pro bono* work as well, mostly on behalf of kids from rouch council estates who'd got unlucky, been busted for first-time possession - drugs, concealed weapons, whatever a random police stop-and-search turned up - or else were facing charges of assault or GBH when they ere only trying to protect themselves or their family.

Those kids, they'd look at me in frank wonder sometimes. Never seen someone with the same skin colour as them who wore a suit and spoke the way I did. "What, you posh or summink, bruv? You Prince Charles or summink? How come you don't talk right?"

No, not posh, I would tell them. I come from the same place you do. Igrew up on the London streets. My parents had no money, same as yours. But I studied hard at school. I went to university on a scholarship and got a Graduate Diploma in Law. I was called to the Bar at Lincoln's Inn. I worked my backside off to make a success of myself.

And you can too.

I *was* a success, I don't mind admitting it. Nice flat in St. John's Wood. Tenancy in well regarded set of chambers based near the Barbican. Steady and enviable income. I kept myself in trim-weight training twice a week, a jog around Regent's Park every other morning. I kept my home in trim, too. Very house-proud, me. Had that instilled into me by my mum. "A clean home is a good him," she'd say as she hurricaned from room to room with vacuum cleaner and feather duster, hands gauntleted in Marigolds. We had a tiny council flat, and it was always immaculate, not a speck of dust anywhere. My pad in St. John's was the same — spotless. Windows gleaming bright. Floors swept to within an inch of their lives. Bathroom dazzing. Did it all myself, what's more. I could easily afford a cleaner, but nobody else could keep things to my exacting standards. My mother, God rest her soul, would have approved. She cleaned other people's houses for a living and felt no shame in that, but he did believe a person should be responsible for their own domestic hygiene.

"It's your mess. Don't do you no good paying someone else to make it go away."

I can't remember when exactly I noticed the first web. Sometime in midsummer, late July, but I can't be any more precise than that. It wasn't big, covering one windowpane. Flick of a dustcloth and it was gone.

The second appeared a couple of days later, stretched between a bookcase and the ceiling cornice. Bigger than the first, but just as easily got rid of.

The flat had never been troubled b spiders before. Insufficient prey. Flies and their ilk didn' flourish at my place. Not enough of the dirt and debris they thrived on.

A week passed, and one day I came home and there were a good half-dozen webs. They hadn't been there when I'd left that morning. One was draped around the light fixture in the living room. One linked the kitchen sink taps to the drying rack. One neatly filled the ring-seat on the toilet.

They were beautiful webs, I have to give them that. Pristine. Exactly how you imagine a spider web should look. The radial strands neatly equidistant, the concentric rings laddering out at steadlily larger intervals, as though according to some fundamental mathematical principle. A certain silveriness to the silk, a gossamer iridescence. If they'd been anywhere else, anywhere but my home, I'd have admired them, marvelled at them.

As it was, I eradicated them. Angrily. Then I called in a pest control company.

The man in the Bug Blasterz overalls searched and searched, but couldn't find any trace of spider infestation.

"No eggs," he said. "No cocoons. No husks. Nothing. You're sure they were webs?"

"Yes, I'm damn well sure they were webs," I replied sharply. "What else would they have been?"

"Only asking."

He squirted insect repellent everywhere and advised me to stay outdoors for at least three hours. When I returned, the flat reeked of chemicals but felt somehow purified, as though I'd had ghosts and a priest had come and exorcised them.

My orderly life resumed. For a fortnight, my routine was as it had ever been. Work, fitness, cleaning, sleep. I found time to go on a date—a blind date set up by a well-meaning colleague, who thought I was working too hard and not "playing" enough. She was a nice enough girl, a solicitor, petite but curvy where it counts. West Indian, though, and sorry, I can't help it, but my parents' prejudices are my own. I remember my dad saying, "The stupid ones got caught. The clever ones knew how to run and hide. Those slave traders did Africa a favour, leaving the best and taking the rest." It's not true; what many of the clever Africans did was sell their countrymen to the slave traders. That's how they survived. But we all tell lies to ourselves about our ancestors, to make us feel better, and those lies are persuasive.

So the date ended with a polite peck on the cheek and me about a hundred and fifty quid out of pocket for dinner at a Michelin-starred restaurant.

And I got in that night to find my flat *swathed* in spider webs. Literally hundreds of them. Spider webs everywhere.

It was like some sort of practical joke. As though a prankster had broken in and gone mad with those spray cans they use to make cobwebs on movie sets. I couldn't move without sticky silk wrapping itself around my hands, my legs, my head. I scarsely dared breathe for fear of getting some of the stuff in my mouth or up my nose.

This is insane, I thought. *This can't be happening.*

I took myself in hand, told myself to get a grip. It was just spider webs. Just dirt that shouldn't be there. I fought my way through the webs to the cleaning cupboard and fetched out dustcloths, broom, brush, dustpan, Dyson upright and Mr. Sheen, then tied a bandanna over the lower half of my face and set to work. I took the best part of two hours, but by midnight I'd got the job done. Not a scrap of web remained. It was all inside a pair of large black bin bags, which were stuffed full but weighed nest to nothing and which I dumped in the wheelie bin outside with equal parts satisfaction and irritation. Bug Blasterz would be getting a very stern phone call in the morning. You do not bill Dion Yeboah £175 plus VAT for "services rendered" if said services have patently not been rendered.

●●●

In the middle of the night I woke to find a huge spider squatting on my chest.

It was black against the pale bedcovers, lit by the streetlight glow coming through the curtains. Its carapace glinted dully. Eight long legs straddled my torso, their outermost tips reaching from my collarbone to my navel and fron one side of my ribcage to the other.

I lay there in a paroxysm of horror. It was the biggest, blackest, ugliest spider I'd ever laid eyes on. I didn't dare move. I had an urge to hurl the thing off me, but at the same time I didn't want to alarm it, provoke it. What if it was venomous? A spider that size—if it bit me it would surely kill me.

A dozen shiny eyes regarded me carefully. The mandibles beneath them rustled and clicked, mouth parts folding in and out of one another with machinelike precision.

Dion.

A voice. A whisper inside my mind.

Dion Yeboah. I am here for you. I have come for you.

I woke again. I was still in bed, still on my back, bathed in fear sweat. But there was no spider. No giant black arachnid perched on top of me, gazing at me with myriad jet-coloured eyes.

I'd dreamed it, of course. Spiders had overrun my flat with their webs earlier in he evening, so naturally I'd had a spider-themed nightmare.

Made perfect sense.

I didn't sleep again that night, however. Not a wink.

Mr. Bug Blasterz came back and did the same as before, namely doubt the veracity of my claims and souse the flat with poison. At least he had the good sense not to invoice me for the cost of the repeat visit.

The following night, the spider returned.

Dion, it said.

I had no doubt that the whisper I was hearing inside my head — a mental tickling that was as much sensation as sound — was the spider's voice.

Dion, I have come far. I have travelled thousands of miles to find you. I have chosen you, you out of the many I could have chosen to be mine.

"Who are you?" I challenged that black monstrosity. Its face, if you could call it a face, was just inches from mine.

Who am I? Its mandibles flared. I heard a raspy chuckle. *Oh, you know who I am, Dion. You know full well. I am he whom your grandmother told you about all those years ago. I am Kwaku Ananse. I am Ananse-Tor. I am Nansi. I am Kuent'I Nanzi. I am Ayiyi. I am the god of countless names and countless stories. Everything your Nanabaa Oboshie told you, that is who I am.*

"What do you want?" I demanded. "Why are you here? Why me?"

I want to be with you, said Anansi. *I want your story to become mine and mine yours. I want our tales to intertwine. I want us to be together. We have work to do.*

"Work? What work?"

Let me in, Dion. Let me inside you. See what we ccand do together, the two of us. See what we can achieve.

"No!" I cried. "No! Leave me alone! I don't believe in you. You're just a myth. An African old wives' tale. A story for children. I have nothing to do with you. You don't belong in my world."

Let's just see about that, said Anansi. *Let's just see.*

Things started to go wrong.

Nothing major, on the face of it. I missed the bus to work a couple of mornings in a row, or rather, the bus failed to turn up as scheduled. The second time, I walked to Edgware Road and took the Tube instead, only for the train to get held up in the tunnel for an hour—a suicide farhter down the line, apparently. So I was late to into chambers both those mornings, and late to court. Everything was a rush, but I compensated. None of my clients was short-changed and the verdicts ran the right way.

Then a case I'd been nurturing for weeks and feeling confident about suddenly veered off-course and seemed headed for disaster. We were ready to go to trial, but a key witness changed his testimony, deciding almost on a whim that he *had* seen the accused commit violence at the pub that night after all, removing a vital plank in our defence. I scrambled to find someone who could shore things up for us again. Eventually I convinced a lesser witness to be, shall we say, more certain about her facts than she had been previously. I managed to gloss over the discrepancies between her statement in court in such a way that the jurors hardly seemed to notice any difference. Busy, crowded pub. Alcohol imbibed. Under those circumstances, recollections are often clearer some weeks later than they are in the immediate aftermath of the event. Skin of my teeth, but I pulled it off, and our man walked free.

Then I got word from various mutual acquaintances that the girl I'd gone on that blind date with had begun making disparaging remarks about me. She was saying I'd behaved badly, been rude, snobby, insulting, even racist. It was absurd, of course. I might have been somewhat distracted that evening, maybe not paying her as much attention as she thought she merited, and possibly I'd alluded to the West Indies once or twice in less than complimentary terms, but snobby? Racist? Preposterous. I phoned her to straighten the matter out. She maintained that she'd been misquoted. I suggested that if she was unhappy with the way the evening had panned out, there were better ways of dealing with her disappointment than bandying slanderous accusations about. The conversation didn't end on a positive note, but I felt that I got my point across.

Little things. Minor annoyances. In and of themselves, nothing much.

But this sort of stuff simply did not happen to Dion Yeboah. I organised my life precisely so that there would be a minimum of grief and disruption. I worked hard to maintain my routine and keep everything on an even keel.

I did not like my shipshape little boat being rocked.

"Anansi," I said to my empty flat. "I know you don't exist. I know you're not listening to me. But—if you *are* there..."

Silence. Only the murmur of traffic outside and the purr of the refrigerator.

"If you *are* there, please go away. Please stop interfering. I've done nothing to deserve this. All I wish is to be allowed to carry on as before. I've done nothing wrong, nothing to offend you. Find somebody else to bother. Leave me be."

I felt foolish, talking to thin air, addressing a spider deity who had appeared to me in dreams alone. I wished Nanabaa Oboshie was with me, so that she could confirm that I had only imagined Anansi. "A story, a story." That was all he was. Nanabaa Oboshie knew that. Much though my grandmother had loved to tell me of Anansi's escapades—his silly stunts that almost always backfired, the tricks he played and the trouble they got him into with his fellow gods and the other animals—she was perfectly well aware that he was a fiction. She herself had learned the tales from her own grandmother back in Ghana, sitting in the wattle-walled hut, by the fire. Anansi existed solely as oral tradition handed down from generation to generation, a way to entertain the tribe on a dark hot night while the lions roared in the hills.

Anansi certainly did not have a place in twenty-first century London, in the flat of a sophisticated and highly intelligent lawyer.

I kept insisting on this to myself even after the improbably large black spider descended in front of me from the ceiling, suspended from a delicate thread of silk.

So you believe now, do you? Anansi said.

"I don't know what to believe," I said, hesitantly. The truth.

Good. An open mind. That's progress. But you mustn't be afraid, Dion. Above all else, not that. I shouldn't frighten you. I'm here to help.

"Help? How?"

If you'll just accept me – fully, wholeheartedy – then you'll see.

"Accept?"

Am I real?

"You – you *look* real."

Think how you could know for sure.

I thought. I studied the spider's fat round abdomen, the wormy spinnerets that extruded the thread, the tiny hairs fringing the legs.

"I coud touch you," I said.

Touch me, then, said Anansi. *Feel my solidity. There will be your proof.*

I was repulsed by the idea. Who would want to touch a spider that size? Who in their right mind would want to go anywhere near it? Even Sir David

Attenborough would think twice.

My hand went out, shrank back, several times. Anansi hung there, patient, waiting.

Finally, in a mad dash of bravado, I brushed my fingers against the creature's back.

For the briefest of moments, barely a millisecond, I felt *something*. The coolness of chitin. The hardness of a living shell.

That was all it took.

The spider vanished.

But it wasn't gone.

Anansi was within me. I felt him there as surely as I could feel my heartbeat, the air passing in and out of my nostrils, the gurgling of my digestive system. I had allowed Anansi in, and now he was a part of me.

Yes, Anansi said. *Yes, that's better. That's so much better, isn't it, Dion?*

I nodded. I could hardly speak.

So let's go and have some fun, said Anansi. *You and me. I'm looking forward to this.*

Read about Dion's adventures with Anansi in AGE OF ANANSI.

Separate from the Animals

By Jason Evans

Like you, Jason Evans is not yet a New York Times bestselling novelist, but he'll buy your book if you'll buy his. While his day job as a corporate trainer pays the bills, he prefers to spend time writing science fiction and fantasy and likes to believe his regular public speaking will serve him well on future book tours. Jason lives in Naperville, Illinois, with his wife, daughter, and an assortment of dogs.

Papa was ranting about the spiders again.

Celeste wished she could burrow into the thin foam cushions of the collapsible futon and disappear. She scrunched herself back as far as she could and tried to focus on her art homework on her tablet. When they started the lesson Mama had told her 'Art is what separates us from the animals,' but right now she envied Joey, sleeping peacefully in her dog bed under the futon.

Mama pulled Papa into their bedroom and slid shut the folding door. "Hush, now. Celeste will hear and get scared!"

Mama meant well, but it was a little late for that. The shelter hut was so small she could always hear them, and Papa talked about the spiders every day. They didn't have to worry about spiders the size of dogs back on Earth (big ones, like wolves, not little ones like Joey) and here she didn't even have her own room to hide in. The huts had been carried down from the colony ship in the landing rocket, so everything was small and light and felt like cheap plastic. She slept on the futon, so that made the squished together living room and kitchen her bedroom. The water closet connected to Mama and Papa's bedroom, and there weren't any other rooms.

Papa said he'd build them a real house as soon as the settlement was stable. He said the big red trees with the spiky purple leaves were really good for building; that the wood was as strong as oak but grew fast like bamboo. And he promised once he burned the wood with his beamer the veins would stop leaking tree juice, and then some white paint would cover the pink tree meat and it wouldn't be like living inside a dead body at all. Not one bit.

Celeste switched to the art app on her tablet and looked over her latest drawing. Her house looked good, her old one, back on Earth, with the treehouse in the yard just like she remembered. But the tree itself wasn't quite right. They'd only been on this planet a couple of months, but the green leaves in her drawing already looked weird. And did Earth trees have the pink veins running up their trunks, or was that just the trees here?

From the bedroom, Papa's voice carried through the flimsy door. "The damn spiders ate Henri's foot! Took it clean off with those pincers they've got. Didn't even know the thing was there until he stepped in its hole and fell onto it."

Mama kept her voice low, said something soothing, but Papa's voice just got louder.

"If I hadn't beamed it that thing would have eaten him whole! It's not bad enough they're tearing up our crops, now they're eating us, too! They're monsters, Marie! Monsters!"

Celeste tried to cover her ears with her shoulders, then gave up and flipped closed her tablet cover.

"Mama, I'm going outside!" she called toward the bedroom door. She preferred to stay inside, of course, where the spiders for sure couldn't get her, but she couldn't listen to Papa anymore. Besides, the spiders had never gotten inside the repulsor fence. Even Papa said they were safe inside.

"All right, Little Star, but stay close. And finish your art homework!"

Celeste rolled her eyes as she stuffed her tablet into her backpack. "I know, Mama. 'Art is what makes us human.'"

Mama slid open the door. "Well, it's true. You don't see Josephine doing any painting, do you?"

At the sound of her name, Joey's black head popped out from under the futon, round eyes bulging. Tongue lolling and curly tail wagging so hard her whole body vibrated, the little Chihuahua scurried over and rolled to her back at Mama's feet, exposing her pink belly for scratching. Despite Papa grumbling behind her, Mama smiled.

Celeste triggered the door opener and slipped out as it slid open, "Come on, Joey. Let's go find something to draw. Do you want to learn to draw, Joey? Do you want to draw?" Joey bounced with excitement and sprinted off, Celeste in hot pursuit.

They headed for the hill on the west side of the settlement. It wasn't much of a hill, really, but it stood higher than the shelters. The top was bare except for the antenna cluster, and it made a good place to see the whole settlement.

Atop the hill, she pulled her tablet and a treat for Joey from her backpack and looked for something new to draw. The modular shelters were super boring. It was hard to even pick out her hut from here as the dull gray rows all looked the same. The different flower shapes were pretty, but she was tired of always coloring everything purple. The mountains were boring during the day. They'd be better at sunset when the snow on top glowed all pink and gold. Outside the east gate, a farm crew in their green coveralls used tillers to make rows in the red dirt for new seedlings. To the north, a survey team wearing orange moved way out in the lavender brush on the far side of the landing rocket. She'd already drawn the rocket a bunch, but it was still weird to see it from the outside. It felt so tiny inside, but looked so big sitting in the field! The silver cylinder towered over the piles of red dirt Papa called termite mounds, and even over the twisting violet vines that snaked up into the sky in clusters of eight.

The two suns overhead gave the rocket two shadows. They gave everything two shadows. Mama she said the extra shadows made her dizzy, but Celeste loved them. She dropped her backpack and danced, the twinned shadows of her arms and legs flowing behind. Joey rose on her rear legs and hopped around as well, corkscrew tail wagging. Laughing, Celeste plopped to the ground and scratched the dog's head.

Joey's ears perked up as someone in the farm crew yelled in the distance. A hurt yell, like when Papa hit his thumb with the hammer and it got all black and the thumbnail fell off. Celeste craned her neck to see. Several of the men huddled together at the edge of the new field among all the purple plants, waving their arms and jumping around like silly gooses. One of the men drew his beamer and pointed it at the ground until a trickle of smoke drifted up. Celeste watched as a couple of the farmers lifted up a third and walked back to the gate with the third man hopping between them.

Behind her, Joey barked. Celeste turned and finally saw something new and colorful — a balloonerfly drifting by the antenna! Fluttering its stubby wings with their bright stripes of green and yellow beneath its vivid blue air sack, it landed in a patch of wildflowers, the little knobby plum ones that tasted like honey. Celeste scratched Joey's head again and opened her tablet to sketch, sitting crisscross applesauce on the ground so Joey could snuggle on her lap.

She'd only finished drawing three of its four pairs of wings when the balloonerfly took off, striped wings beating until it rose high enough to inflate its air sack. Then the breeze took it, carrying it down the hill and toward the repulsor fence on the west side of the settlement.

"No! Come back balloonerfly! I didn't draw your head yet!" She grabbed her backpack and ran after it.

The balloonerfly rocked beneath its air sack as the wind gusted, sailed over the repulsor fence, and dropped, wings aflutter, deflating its membrane and landing in a new patch of magenta flowers with coral veins lining their broad petals. Celeste stopped and groaned as she neared the fence, jumping up and stretching on her tiptoes, trying to get a better view through the green blur of the repulsor field. This close, the repulsor field raised the hair on her arms.

"Oh! It's so close, Joey! I just can't see it through the stupid fence." She backpedaled up the hill until she could see over the fence and resumed her drawing, tongue sticking out with concentration, squinting to see the details. Joey sniffed around, examining each clump of grass and marking them as her own. She tried to mark the fence was well, but jumped away with a yip when she edged too close.

Again the balloonerfly's air sack inflated and it drifted with the breeze, floating along the fence line before dipping out of sight into some purple weeds just outside the west gate.

"Come on, Mr. Balloonerfly! I just need a few more minutes!"

Frowning, she walked to the gate. There was no one else around. The other gates had lots of activity during the day as the work teams went in and out, but tucked away behind the hill and not yet developed outside, the west gate didn't see much traffic. She bit her lip and peered carefully through the green blur at the low brush nearby.

"It's right there, Joey." She looked around again. "The spiders can't get us as long as we stay inside the fence, right? And it just takes a second to close the gate if we see something coming. Keep your eyes open, Joey."

She raised her tablet, typed Mama's access code (Mama never covered the tablet when she signed in; Celeste couldn't help that she'd seen the code) and deactivated the gate. The shimmering green of the repulsor field disappeared. She waited, finger poised over the activation button. Nothing. After another look around she leaned out, bending from the waist and careful to keep her feet inside the fence, until she could see the balloonerfly in all its glory.

"See, Joey. We're safe here." She resumed her sketch.

A few seconds later, a strong gust of wind lifted the blue air sack skyward, and the balloonerfly drifted down the trail away from the settlement.

Celeste stomped her feet with frustration. "Stupid bug! I didn't want to draw you anyway!" She pouted, lower lip jutting, and reached for the button to close the gate. With an outburst of rapid barks, Joey ran between past her, through the gate and out into the purple brush.

"Joey!"

Ahead of Joey, deeper in the weeds, something moved, skittering away from them. Joey darted into the undergrowth in pursuit.

"Joey! No, bad! Come!"

Joey ran farther and farther from the gate, yapping, tracking the movement. Celeste jammed her tablet into her backpack and gave chase, following as Joey ran toward a cluster of the violet vines.

"Joey! Come! Treats!" Celeste saw something pink dash into a small hole at the base of the vines. Barking wildly, Joey disappeared into the hole in pursuit.

"Joey!" Celeste sprinted to the edge of the hole and peered in, pulling away a matted bunch of purple and blue grasses that hid a larger opening. The hole led into a crude round tunnel, less than a meter high, dug into the red dirt and descending into darkness.

Joey's barks still sounded ahead. As her eyes adjusted, Celeste could just make out Joey's tail and hindquarters bouncing in and out of sight around a bend a couple of meters down the tunnel. Joey squeaked and leaped back, barely dodging a snapping red pincer twice the size of her whole body. A loud crack reverberated down the tunnel as the pincer closed, then Joey darted back in, growling with all ferocity her tiny body could muster.

"Joey! Come back! It's spiders!" Celeste called, voice tight with fear. "Please, someone help!" She shouted back the way they'd come, but she couldn't even see the gate. No one could hear her cries.

She ducked into the tunnel.

Enclosed and reflected by the smooth dirt walls, Joey's barks stabbed into Celeste's ears. Wincing, she scrabbled forward on hands and knees, fingers gouging the red soil. Joey jumped and the pincer snapped again as Celeste crawled closer.

"Joey, come! Please!" she cried, reaching for the little dog. The tunnel got even darker around the bend, but as she approached she could just make out eyes glittering in the light. Lots of eyes. The pincer snapped,

Joey sprang back, and Celeste lunged forward, grabbing Joey's curly pigtail and hauling the dog to her. She squeezed Joey tight against her chest and backed up the tunnel as quickly as she could with one arm clamping down the dog's wriggles. In the tunnel, the spider hissed and advanced around the turn.

For all that papa talked about them, she hadn't seen a spider up close before. It was big. Not just big for a spider, but really big. Bigger than Papa when he got down on all fours and let her ride horsey back. So big its sides brushed the walls of the tunnel. It hissed and clicked, shivering and ruffling the shaggy maroon hair covering its back, then reared up, exposing its pale pink underbelly and brandishing its four pincer arms. Clusters of bulbous eyes covered it, grouped in sets of four and gleaming darkly. Not just big eyes on its face, but all over. On its shoulders. On its chest. Small eyes even glinted on the base of its abdomen, where its spider butt would be. It snapped its four pincers, crashing the eight ends together. The pincers weren't hairy. Their slick shells stuck out from the hair of the arms like ax heads ready to chop her up.

She screamed, kicking and pulling against the dirt walls, scraping her knees and shoulders as she struggled to escape, to make it back to the circle of light at the tunnel entrance. Then that light went dark. Another spider stood just outside the entry.

Celeste stopped. She couldn't breathe. She couldn't think. Even Joey went quiet. The spider in the tunnel hissed again, so close its breath washed over her, warm and moist and sweet like honey. She was trapped. She rocked back against the wall and pressed her face down onto Joey.

131

"I'm sorry, Joey! I shouldn't have opened the gate!" Joey's tongue flicked against her cheeks, licking her tears. To either side of her, so close she could reach out and touch them, the spiders chittered and hissed, pincers swaying in the air. But not snapping closed and chopping her up.

Suppressing a sob, she ventured a glance at the one deeper in the tunnel. It had backed off a pace and stood, hairy flanks shivering and twitching, still chittering. Its pincer arms drifted downward, pulling back toward its body. The spider near the entrance clicked and whistled. Shaggy hair covered it as well, but blue and purple spots mottled its red coat, like an apple covered in bruises. The maroon one in the tunnel whistled back. They weren't eating her.

As she watched, even more eyes opened on the maroon spider, dozens of them. Some began to fall off, dropping from the hair like dandruff made of eyeballs. Celeste stared, wanting to gag but unable to look away as pink bunches of eyes rolled on the floor, turned themselves upright, and stared back at her.

Her hands trembling, she reached into her backpack and drew out the tablet. When she tapped on the screen light, the spiders flinched and hissed, but now she saw their eyes hadn't fallen out. The tunnel swarmed with little spiders, some the size of Joey, others even smaller like little pale plums. Babies! The baby spiders, covered in peach-fuzz pink fur, skittered toward her, chittering and hissing as they followed the light. Joey growled and tried to squirm free. Celeste gave her a squeeze and a "tsst!" and she settled down. At the sound, the spiders quieted, too. They watched her, heads cocked.

"Um, hello?" Her voice cracked and wavered. The maroon spider whistled and the babies fled behind it, some scampering back up its legs and concealing themselves in its fur. Her lips stuck and her tongue felt wrapped in cotton, but she forced herself to speak. "I'm sorry my dog chased your baby, mama spider. We didn't mean to scare you."

The spiders chittered and clicked. The spotted one by the entrance twitched and Celeste closed her eyes tight, waiting for the pincer. When it didn't come, she dared a look. The spider had moved back outside, clearing the entrance. She decided it must be the papa.

"Joey, I don't think they're going to eat us," she whispered. Joey quivered and licked her chin. Held tight against her side, Joey's tail sprang to life, tickling Celeste's ribs. Moving slowly, Celeste slid off her backpack, opening it enough to push Joey inside. Joey squirmed and twisted until her head popped out of the top of the bag. Celeste fastened the opening up to Joey's neck, snug enough to keep her inside, then slipped the pack on. Eyes locked on the spiders, she scooted, one slow move at a time, toward the daylight. As she approached, papa spider stepped back, giving her room. The eyes on its body moved, more babies readjusting their positions in papa's shaggy hair. With one last slide Celeste exited the tunnel, brushing bits of loose soil from her knees.

"Thank you," she said to papa spider. "Thank you," she repeated down the tunnel. "Joey, let's—" She stopped as she noticed marks on the tunnel wall, just inside the entrance. She hadn't seen them before, but now, sitting just outside the hole, they were obvious. Not just marks. Drawings. The tunnel wall, from entrance to as far as she could see into the dark, was covered in drawings. The forms were angular and jagged, but she recognized an outline of the mountains with two suns above. A vine tree. Small sketches of the spiders themselves. And there, at the very lip of the hole, the landing rocket with its jutting fins and oval windows, towering over termite mounds. On the floor of the tunnel, scattered by her movements, sat small pile of flat-edged rocks and long magenta leaves, tightly curled and pointed like sticks. Tools for drawing in the dirt. She pushed a bit of the grass mat cover aside and looked closer.

Papa spider hissed, pincers raised.

"Wait! You draw?" She pointed to the real rocket in the distance, and to the image scratched into the wall. "I draw, too. Look." She raised her tablet, moving carefully, and flipped the screen from her half-finished balloonerfly to one of her own rocket drawings. She turned the tablet so papa spider could see the screen. It hissed, its warm, honey breath flowing over her, then cocked its head and leaned in, looking intently at the screen. Several of the babies hanging from it looked too.

She slid the stylus from the case, flipped to a new drawing screen, and began to sketch papa spider, holding the tablet so it could see her work. The spider whistled and chittered. Mama spider scuttled closer, babies dropping free and skittering around. Celeste froze as two of them clambered over her feet, pausing and rushing like lizards, on their way to papa spider. Mama spider reached out a pincer, delicately lifted a rolled leaf brush and dragged it against the wall. The spider drew choppily, jerking the tool from place to place, but after a few moments the effect was undeniable. The spider was drawing Celeste. A crude portrait, but clearly a person, and with the round head and bulging eyes of a nervous Chihuahua peeking up over her shoulder. With its other pincer mama spider reached down and scooped up a baby. It placed the baby in the hair of its back, mirroring Celeste and Joey.

"You draw!" Eyes wide, she looked from one spider to the other, to the babies, to the drawings. "But Papa says you're monsters. That you're dangerous animals. He burned the one that attacked Uncle Henri." She gasped, throwing her hand to her mouth. "Uncle Henri fell into a hole. Into a nest! Papa killed a mama trying to defend her babies!" Fresh tears leaked onto her cheeks. "I'm sorry! We didn't know!"

Mama spider clicked and whistled, paused, then repeated the noises. It cocked its head and watched Celeste.

"I know you're talking, but I don't understand." She held up her tablet and flipped to a new screen, but hesitated. What could she draw to explain to them?

Mama spider clicked again, then used her hairy side to wipe smooth a section of the tunnel wall. Baby spiders scrambled to reposition themselves on her back. She picked up one of the rocks and carved in the dirt. Celeste scooted back into the tunnel and sat down her tablet, angling it so the light shined on the wall where mama spider worked. Mama spider first drew upright cones, then thick lines snaking upwards—the termite mounds and vines. Around them she added blobs with eight legs, many of them. Mama spider stopped, looking at Celeste, and tapped the wall.

"It's you and your family, your people, living here. I understand." She pointed outside, then to the spiders and babies, then to the wall.

Mama spider whistled. Its honey breath gusted in Celeste's face, but it must have been satisfied as it returned to drawing. It added a tall cylinder to the scene, then windows and fins.

"Yes! We came here in the rocket." Celeste tapped her own chest, and then Joey's bobbing head.

Mama spider squeaked and chittered, snapping her pincers in the air. Papa spider snapped as well. Mama lashed out with both pincers, gouging at the wall, scraping away the spider figures, the mounds, even the trees until only the rocket remained, surrounded by destruction. Atop it all, she drew a stick figure. A person standing triumphant among the ruins of the spider's world.

Celeste reached out and touched the wall, red dirt crumbling away from her fingers. "We were clearing the land for fields. For food, so we could eat. We didn't know you were smart. That you draw. That you're people."

One of the baby spiders stirred on mama's back. It stretched its legs, one pair at a time, then leaped, landing on Celeste's arm. Joey barked and the baby hissed. Mama plucked it off and sat it down next to Celeste's feet. It scuttled over to the tablet and poked at the bright screen.

Palms up, Celeste lowered her cupped hands beside the baby. It hopped on, eight legs and pink fuzz tickling as it explored her fingers. It closed a tiny pincer on her finger, squeezing and releasing.

"We thought you were monsters."

She lowered the baby spider to the floor, then reached out and smoothed over the ruined section of mama's drawing. Taking up a pointed leaf, she re-drew the spider figures, alongside the person.

"I'll tell everyone. Once they know, we can all live here together."

Behind her, papa spider screeched. It reared up, chittering and clacking its pincers, then collapsed to its side, mottled hair bursting into flame. Baby spiders fell from it, some running, some charred and unmoving. The stench of burning hair filled the tunnel, choking Celeste. Joey squirmed and struggled, barking madly. From outside, between barks, Celeste heard shouting.

" —a tunnel!"

" —sphine barking!" Her Mama's voice, shrill and frightened.

"Celeste!" Papa's voice, loud and angry.

"No!" she screamed. "No! Papa!" Celeste dove for the entrance, squinting against the suns as a farm worker in green kicked aside the spider's burning body. She reached for it, for the babies still hanging on the corpse, but her Papa was there, beamer in hand. He grabbed her arm and yanked her out of the hole, shoving her back toward Mama and another farm worker. Mama grabbed her, lifting Celeste into her arms, weeping as she hugged her tight. At the entrance hole, Papa crouched down, beamer pointed into the tunnel.

"NO!" Celeste screamed. "Papa!"

"Fucking spiders!" Papa fired the beamer. Mama spider screeched, echoed by the tiny whistles of the babies. Smoke drifted from the burrow.

"Papa! Stop!"

He swept the beamer back and forth. Baby spiders popped and crackled, pink fuzz blackening as they burned.

Celeste gasped and choked, tears pouring from her eyes in a torrent of heartbreak.

"It's OK, Celeste. You're safe." Mama stroked her hair and turned her away from the carnage of the spider hole.

"No, Mama!" Celeste gasped. "They're people, Mama! They make art! They're not animals, they're people!"

Mama's brow creased, but then Papa was there, pulling Celeste up with his strong arms, examining her for injuries.

"I think we got her in time. I don't see any blood."

"Papa, they're people! They have drawings!"

"She's in shock. Let's get her home. Doc's on his way with the other search teams." He turned and stalked off, cradling Celeste against his chest.

"No, Papa, wait!" She squirmed and struggled like Joey in her pack, but couldn't break his grip.

"Mama! My tablet! Look at their art!" Celeste popped an arm free and pointed at the tunnel. Mama looked down the tunnel, beamer raised. The tablet light still glowed inside.

"Wait, Jacques," Mama said. "We need to get it. We can't get her a new one."

Papa paused, motioned for the farmers to cover Mama with their beamers.

Straining to keep her head above Papa's shoulder, Celeste watched as Mama took a deep breath against the smoke, dropped to her belly, and reached into the tunnel. The tablet light slid across the walls as she drew it out. Mama gasped and the tablet light stopped, then scanned back across the tunnel walls.

"Oh my God." Mama stood, eyes wide, staring at Celeste. She pointed into the tunnel. "Jacques, look at this."

Celeste collapsed against Papa's chest and wept. Smoke tinged the air, making her eyes burn. In the tunnel, the spiders' art danced in the flickering light of their smoldering bodies.

The Courtship Dance

By Jennifer Lee Rossman

Jennifer Lee Rossman is science fiction geek who is afraid of all spiders, unless they're pretty and know how to dance. Her time travel novella *Anachronism* is now available from Grimbold Books, and her debut novel, *Jack Jetstark's Intergalactic Freakshow*, will be published by World Weaver Press in December.

She blogs at jenniferleerossman.blogspot.com and tweets @JenLRossman

Outer space was, to use a highly technical astrophysics term, absolutely freaking awesome.

There were many reasons humanity had reached for the stars, ranging from exploration and mining to the very real possibility that humanity would one day render Earth totally unable to support life. But mostly, Judith decided as she watched Jupiter swirling outside her bedroom window like a giant creamy candy, it was the awesomeness factor.

Space made everything graceful. You couldn't fall, you couldn't drop things. Everyone became a ballerina in zero-G, twirling weightless and unencumbered.

Even her body, clumsy and chubby and with its atrophied muscles that couldn't bear their own weight back home, worked like everyone else's. Just a simple push off the wall, and off she went, gliding free until she encountered an object with more inertia.

Judith spent every spare moment doing just that,

trying to move faster, fling herself farther each time. She'd come to space to work on the ship's engineering deck, but now that she was there, she wanted to *dance*.

Not the ballet and classic waltzes Arabella taught in the exercise classes down on Deck Seven. No. Judith wanted disco, modern, jazz. The kind of wild, exciting moves where dancers flung their limbs like trees in a hurricane, flouncy dresses spinning and billowing.

You know. *Dance*.

Her favorite Prince song rocked from her speakers, shaking the steel walls of her quarters and reverberating through the spiderwebs in the corner. No one else on the ship enjoyed her centuries-old music, but Judith couldn't get enough of the era of day-glo and side ponytails.

She pressed her back to the wall, tensing every muscle while she waited for the chorus, then flung her limbs back to propel herself forward with as much strength as she could muster.

In her mind, she was an explosion of movement and energy, striking a dramatic pose as the music hit its little red crescendo. In reality, however, she merely drifted across the room at a brisk pace, and with nothing to stop her forward momentum, her attempt at a dramatic pose tipped her upside down as she gently collided with the wall.

"Blast," she muttered, pouting as her spider hovered in front of her face on a gossamer filament.

In the silence between songs, Judith heard a steady rhythm outside her door that her brain first labeled as footsteps, but no one walked in space. More likely, it was the sound of someone pulling themselves along the handles installed in the hallway for just that purpose.

"Blast again."

She scrambled to shut off the music and smooth out her dress--a futile act in zero-G, but, like the title of the songfic she'd written in high school about John MacLean teaming up with an aging nun said, Old Habits Die Hard--and opened the door as soon as he knocked.

"Hey," Ian said, turning himself upside down to match her current orientation. He was a pretty man, all long legs and floppy hair, with a smile that rivaled the stars in brightness. "You, ah... Do you know you have a spider in your hair?"

"Yes," Judith lied with confidence, never considering that it might be more odd to *knowingly* have a spider in your hair than it was to be unaware of it.

He reached out with his prosthetic hand--the same deep brown as his skin, but with rainbow glitter mixed into the plastic--and untangled the web from her curls. Though he did so gently, Judith's chest tightened and she intercepted the dangling spider, pulling her close out of fear of her tiny friend being squooshed.

"Her name's Anita," she said awkwardly, the floating spider tethered to her hand like an astronaut on a spacewalk. "She's an orb-weaver. Not sure what subspecies yet; I'm going to download a book next time we're near a satellite."

Ian nodded slowly. "Is she from the gardening deck?"

"*Maybe.*"

...By which Judith meant *definitely*. That deck was the only one on the ship that had animal life. Insects, mostly, to pollinate the crops that sustained the hundred-and-some-odd people aboard, and some spiders and birds to keep the insect population in check. But she wasn't sure whether it would be frowned upon to steal a spider, so she didn't want to admit to anything.

If this fazed Ian, he didn't let it show. "Anyway, some of the senior crew are throwing a party to welcome the vyomanauts."

Derived from the Sanskrit word for "sky," a vyomanaut was the Indian equivalent of an astronaut or cosmonaut. The word had been used onboard a lot since the Indian Space Program announced they wanted to send some of their scientists to assist the *Iktomi* crew in building a better communications system.

"And you want me to make my famous fried jalebis?"

"No. Well." He reconsidered. "Yes. But mostly I want you to be my date."

Judith's heart went all fluttery for a second. "Me."

"You."

"Okay." She quickly closed the door in his face before he could reconsider, and twirled in excitement, Anita trailing on her web.

Everything Judith knew about courtship, she had learned from studying spiders. And from watching an old VHS of *Dirty Dancing* over and over and over until it wore out. But mostly it was the spiders.

The majority of the courtship was done by the male. Well, screw that. This was the future--she knew it was *officially* the future, because people lived in space--and she decided it was high time females took the lead.

Of course, it wouldn't all translate to human behavior. She doubted there would be a second date if she tried to eat him at the end of the first date, for example, but the rest of it seemed about right.

Step one: be larger than your competition. Judith hovered in front of her mirror, watching her voluptuous stomach and thighs jiggle long after she stopped moving. She gave Anita a thumbs-up, and imagined the little spider writing something encouraging and fat-positive in her web.

"I'm gorgeous?" She put her hand to her cheek in mock shyness. "Oh, Anita, you flatter me."

Step two: ornamentation. With a little help from the riveting machine she had Frankensteined into a bedazzler, she would have the flashiest dress on the ship. It would say "style," it would scream "sexy." Ideally, it would even yodel "my bright colors indicate that I am a healthy individual who has reached sexual maturity!"

So yeah. Step two, check.

Which just left step three: dance.

Orb-weavers like Anita had a more simple courtship, but Judith's favorite jumping spiders were born to boogie.

They had iridescent flaps on their abdomen, the

colors varying by species but always looking like something off the cover of a Lisa Frank notebook. The male flipped this flap up like a peacock fanning its tail, shook his little spider booty, and waved his fuzzy forelegs in the air like he just didn't care. And then, presumably, came much smooching and rubbing of spinnerets.

Judith felt herself blushing at the very thought. Back on Earth, she'd been too busy getting her engineering degree and training for this mission to pay attention to men. Or people of any gender, really. She was out of practice.

She looked at the web in the corner. "I got this, right?"

"Sure do!" she said in Anita's voice, which she decided was a Russian accent. "You are the prettiest girl on this ship, and he would be lucky to have you. So confident, too, and brilliant. All the other girls are going to be super jealous."

Judith decided to believe the spider, and went to work bedazzling.

She just couldn't move *fast* enough. Weightlessness stole the drama from her dramatic sleeve swishing, and turned her rapid spins into graceful twirls no matter how she tried to speed them up.

She flopped on her bed--which was a feat in and of itself, what with all the straps needed to keep her from floating off--and she sulked.

Logically, Judith knew Ian would feel however he

was going to feel regardless of how she danced, but logic had absolutely no place in hormones. She wanted to dance for him. That was the best way she knew to show him how she felt.

Anita hovered unhelpfully in the corner, like Jennifer Grey before Patrick Swayze showed up.

"Oh, right," Judith said, digging around in her pocket. "I got you a snack." She held up a fly--dead, but still nice and juicy. She closed one eye, lining up the shot, and flicked the treat toward the spider.

It tumbled through the air and plinked off the wall. Anita scurried to the edge of her web, but the fly was out of her reach. She scuttled back and forth a bit, as if judging the distance, and leapt.

The spider sailed through the air, swimming in a graceful doggy-paddle, and latched onto the fly with all eight legs. Momentum carried them both farther from the web, floating all the way to the opposite wall and leading to the tricky task of getting her snack back home.

Judith expected Anita would carry her fly around the perimeter of the room. But as she watched, Anita angled herself to face the web, and produced a silky thread from her spinnerets.

In Earth's gravity, such an action would have had little effect on Anita's momentum. But in zero-G, Newton's second law reigned supreme, and the action of expelling the silk from her back end had the equal and opposite reaction of propelling Anita gently toward her web.

Across the room she went, angling her posterior ever so slightly to adjust her course as she left a nearly invisible trail of silk behind her.

Judith sat upright in bed. Tried to, anyway--she forgot about the straps holding her in.

"Anita," she said, "you're a genius."

A distinctly Bollywood vibe pulsed from the recreation deck as the crew welcomed the vyomanauts, sitar and harmonia music mingling with the aromas of spices and Judith's fried dough jalebis. People danced gracefully, some in colorful saris and some in their everyday silver space clothes.

Judith stood on the periphery, the billowy sleeves and folds of her dress tucked around her in a deliberate way that hid the most vibrant colors inside the pleats. She chatted with some of the newcomers, but most of her attention was on the doorway.

When Ian entered, his arm glittering in the lights, she sucked in a breath. This was it, her big moment.

She put a hand to her necklace, a clear plastic sphere dotted with air holes. Inside, Anita's pedipalps quivered in anticipation.

"Here we go," Judith whispered, and glided forward.

The crowd parted, or maybe she only imagined it did, and she locked eyes with Ian from the center of the dancefloor as the band began an instrumental rendition of "(I've Had) The Time of My Life."

She slowly extended a leg, revealing a flash of pink and the merest twinkle of rhinestones beneath the dull gray of her dress, and tapped the ground with her foot like a spider. Thus began the courtship ritual.

She swayed with a rhythmic purpose, watching as Ian's expression went from confusion to amusement. She had to keep her eyes on him, for if she let herself remember all the other eyes around her, she would be too embarrassed to continue.

The song ramped up, the energetic dance break fast approaching. Judith did a little twirl, her skirts rising gently around her legs. When the music exploded into its frenetic chorus, the part so toe-tapping-irific that not even John Lithgow's character from *Footloose* could resist, Judith flicked her wrists and legs to unfurl the full brilliance of her dress.

Yards upon yards of fabric in every color of the rainbow, suspended weightlessly around her as if floating in water, with sparkles that traced her full figure and trailed like strands of spider silk down her limbs.

She soaked up the oohs and aahs from the crowd, but it was the awe in Ian's eyes that gave Judith the courage to engage the CO_2 canisters strapped to her wrists.

Newton would have been proud of this application of his second law, as the equal and opposite reactions spun Judith faster and faster, until she became little more than a blur of color and motion. She turned off the canisters, gave the floor a gentle kick, and rose up, up, up, still spinning, still moving, never wanting to stop.

But all songs had to end, and she wasn't about to miss her cue.

As the very last note rang out, she altered her arm

position and gave a short burst of CO_2, countering her spin and giving her the opportunity to strike that dramatic pose.

As people applauded, Judith pushed off the ceiling and descended with Anita, like a spider on her silk, into Ian's waiting arms in the most perfect *Dirty Dancing* lift ever executed.

And it was, to use a highly technical astrophysics term, absolutely freaking awesome.

THE END

Webinar: Web Sites

By Steven H Silver

Steven H Silver is an American science fiction fan, bibliographer, publisher, and editor. He has been nominated for the Hugo Award for Best Fan Writer twelve times and Best Fanzine four times without winning. Silver is known as an on-line reviewer and has written several articles for science fiction fanzines, as well as publishing his own annual fanzine *Argentus.*

Boris entered the camera frame the way he always did, descending from the ceiling on a gossamer strand of silk finer than most banana spiders. If the light didn't catch it properly, Boris could look like he was simply hanging in midair. Boris always made sure the light did not catch it properly. He liked the effect.

Before speaking, he glanced at his monitor. Seventeen attendees. That meant three spiders hadn't logged on for the webinar. They had already paid so it didn't really matter to him whether they joined or not, although it was always nice to share his knowledge. He quickly scanned the list to see who wasn't on-line. Billy, Gwen, and Miles were absent. Not entirely surprising.

"I'd like to welcome you to the webinar. Today's topic is on web sites. Before we begin, everyone has been muted. If you have any questions, please use the text box and I'll address them as they come in. That said, if you can hear me, please type a Y in the text box."

Boris waited for a few moments. Seventeen Y's appeared on the side of his screen.

"Very good. Everyone can hear me and all of you know how to use the text box."

That hadn't always been the case. The first week of class, Peter couldn't figure out how to type a question and after class had complained that nobody responded when he asked questions into the microphone.

"OK, let's begin. We'll start by acknowledging that every spider species is going to have its own requirements for what makes the best web site, although there are certain factors that all of us will need to address.

"The first thing we all need are anchor points."

A *click* sounded from the computer and Boris glanced over at the text box. Not even through the first sentence of the first item on his agenda and already a question. Gwerlum. He should have known. Boris quickly read the question.

"Yes, Gwerlum. A spider who is ballooning technically doesn't need an anchor point, although in practice, the spider's own body serves as the anchor point in that situation. The web needs to be connected to something and it remains connected to the spider's spinneret. No, Peter, 'spinneret' is not a 'dirty word,' it is just a part of your body.

"I'd also like to remind you that I do not recommend or condone 'ballooning' or 'kiting' or 'floating' for any one of you. It is dangerous and should only be attempted by professionals. Besides, I think Gwerlum might be the only one small enough to successfully balloon. Not that I'm telling Gwerlum to try ballooning. Insects are supposed to fly through the skies. Spiders are supposed to catch them, not chase them."

Boris was glad Peter was too large to try to balloon. He was the only one of the spiders taking the webinar Boris thought was stupid enough to try it. Gwerlum was most likely pulling Boris's legs with the observation in the first place.

"As I was saying, the first thing we all need are anchor points. The first anchor point can be on any surface you like. I recommend a sturdy branch, a large rock, or perhaps a wall, although we'll talk about walls a little later. You want something that is relatively stable and isn't going to move anywhere. Animals, for instance, are not a good place to establish an anchor.

"Once you determine where your first anchor is, you begin to release a strand of silk, allowing the air currents to carry it to the second anchor point."

Click.

"No, Sonya, you don't always have control over where the second anchor point is going to be, although you'll eventually learn to judge distances and air currents, which will give you a better idea of what anchor options you do have."

Sometimes, it was difficult for Boris to remember that these spiderlings hadn't yet built their first webs, even though some of them might have begun experimenting with spinning. That inexperience, that lack of knowledge, is why he offered this series of webinars. If they knew the information, they wouldn't need him to teach them. And if he thought their questions basic, or jumping the gun, at least they were asking questions and interacting.

"Since we covered basic web construction last week, I'm not really going to go into the mechanics of it today. If you have any questions about it, or need a refresher, please wait until after today's session is over and then send me a note directly. I'm more than happy to go over the materials again to make sure you understand it. If you reach out to me one-on-one, I can also discuss specifics for your species of spider.

"So, back to the topic at hands…"

What was the topic at hands? He was talking about bridging, no, that was last week. Sonya asked about the second anchor point. Yes, anchor points.

"The question we really want to look at this week is how to determine your starting anchor point for your web. I've already mentioned some possible places to consider, but it is easy to say, 'start your web on a tree limb.' It is much more difficult to determine which branch of the tree is the appropriate place to anchor.

"I'm going to open a poll for the next couple minutes to give you a chance to guess which answer is best."

Boris clicked on his computer and his image on the screen was replaced by four choices. While the students read them and texted him their opinions, he took advantage of being off-screen to grab a drink of water. By the time he got back into position, all seventeen of the spiderlings had responded to the poll.

"OK, let's see what we have. Six of you responded 'On the highest branch,' five of you said 'Near a piece of fruit,' four of you said, 'The trunk,' and two of you answered 'None of the above.'

"I'll admit that this was a trick question. The correct answer is really all of the above and none of the above. Where you start building your web should depend on several different criteria and those will vary based on the type of spider you are. We'll take a look at the answers I let you choose from and then I'll point out some other things you need to take into account.

"The trunk is probably the least beneficial place to start your web. It is relatively low to the ground and when you float your bridge, it has few places to attach. If you are lucky, you'll attach to one of the lower branches, which is actually higher than your anchor point. More likely, you'll attach to the ground or possibly another nearby tree. While neither of those is ideal, you can build a web like that, but if you don't have to start from the trunk, I wouldn't recommend it.

"Fruit has a tendency to attract insects. By building our web near a piece of fruit, you increase the number of insects that have the opportunity to become ensnared in your web. Building near a piece of fruit is a good option and plays into something I'll cover in a moment.

"If you start your web from the highest branch of a tree, you have the most opportunities for the other end of your bridge to attach, but your web is in a rather random location. It might be easy to build, but that doesn't mean you'll catch any flies.

"Before we continue, I'm going to show you some pictures of spider webs. Some are successful, some are not."

Boris ran a short video. While he was having more to drink, the students were looking at pictures of webs built in various places by various species of spiders. Some of the webs were successful and you could see the trapped flies struggling in the webs. Some were less successful, hanging abandoned when the spider decided to move on. One of them actually showed the corpse of a spider that had failed to move on, but it wasn't obvious and that image didn't stay on the screen for anyone to notice the spider unless they knew exactly when and where to look for it."

A chiming noise interrupted Boris and he glanced over to the side of the screen.

"Billy, so good of you to decide to join us. As usual, a recording of this webinar will be available after today's session is over."

Click.

Sorry I'm late. The reason is kind of embarrassing.

Boris decided to ignore Billy, generally the best response. An immature spiderling for his age, he seemed to feel the web spun around him and he was constantly

155

getting into scrapes that could be easily avoided. If he was offering that his reason for being late was embarrassing, it was only because he craved the attention that would come with asking. Boris expected that Billy has sent the same note to all the others attending the webinar.

"Perhaps none of the above is the correct answer from the choices I gave you, but in reality, the answer is all of the above, plus more. A well fed spider, a fat spider, selects a general area where she wants to build a web and watches it before ever sending out a single strand of silk. Take some time. Keep track of how many midges or flies or gnats, or whatever your favorite prey is, fly through the area. Build your web along their flight paths to capture the greatest amount of food in the shortest amount of time with the least amount of effort.

"In addition to locating the web in a place that has a high exposure to insect migration, it is also important to place your web in an area that isn't going to be disturbed by larger animals. Before I move on to that topic, are there any questions?"

Click.

Mister Boris. Is it possible for a spider to get caught in their own web? Charlotte wrote.

What did that have to do with anything?

"Charlotte, the chances of a spider being caught in its own web are practically zero unless the spider is extremely clumsy and doesn't groom itself properly. Wait. Is Billy claiming he got caught in his own web?"

Click. Click. Click. Click. Click. Click. Click. Click. Click. Click. Click. Click. Click. Click. Click. Click. Click. Click.

Boris looked at the myriad text boxes that suddenly covered his screen. Billy had claimed that he got stuck in his own web.

He let out a sigh.

"This really isn't part of the curriculum and I can't believe I have to address it. If you make sure there is no silk or debris on your legs and are careful to walk on the fine hairs that are on your legs instead of using your actual feet, you won't, you can't, get stuck in your own web. After today's call, I want everyone to practice walking on your hairs."

Click.

Now what?

"Yes, it is possible for a spider to get caught in another spider's web. In fact, some spiders will eat spiders that get caught in their web…"

Click.

"No, it isn't any more disgusting that eating a fly. I don't know of any spiders that will eat a member of their own species under normal circumstances."

Click.

"I don't know. Starvation? Would it be okay with everyone if I get back to the topic? If we have time at the end of the webinar, I can return to this rather morbid topic."

There were no responding clicks, which Boris took to mean he could go back to his topic.

"Now, where was I?"

Click.

Charlotte, of course. *Larger animals.*

"OK, as I was saying, you don't want to build a web where a larger animal is going to walk into it. Sure, you can snare a dog or a chipmunk, but you won't be able to eat the thing and you'll wind up having to build a new nest since the animal will just take the web with it.

"And before you ask, Billy, it would take an eternity for a spider to eat even a small chipmunk.

"But there is one large animal that you should be aware of because they give us additional opportunities. Does anyone know what it is?"

A few clicks. Charlotte, of course, but also Dave and Mina. Boris glanced at their answers.

"Charlotte and Mina, very good. Yes, humans are our best help in deciding where to place our webs, although there are some important caveats to building a web around them.

Click. Billy.

"A caveat is a warning. Something to be aware of when you're choosing a location.

"Humans are unique among the animals in that they build, just like spiders build webs. For many years, there's been debate about whether humans are simply emulating what they see us do, doing it on an instinctive level, or, as some spiders have suggested, have a small level of intelligence that lets them actually build things with thought behind the process. In any event, they do build complex structures, although they don't have the delicacy or structure that even the most simple spider web has. Let's take a look at some of them."

Boris switched the screen over to show a presentation of human structures, all of which supported at least one web.

"Here you can see how spiders have taken advantage of human-spun structures to anchor their webs. You can see that the humans almost instinctively build openings that are symmetrical and just the right size for a spider's web. If you anchor on one of these openings, you are practically guaranteed that your bridge will find a convenient spot to attach.

"These structures, the technical term is 'buildings' can accommodate the smallest webs, like those built by the Samoan moss spiders. Although no Darwin's bark spider webs are known to have been built on a human-spun structure, there is no theoretical reason to believe they couldn't be, although if they did use human buildings, they would probably connect their web between two separate structures."

The presentation ended and Boris looked directly into the camera lens. He knew that if the spiderlings were looking at their monitors it would give the impression that he was making eye contact with them, a useful effect to draw their attention to what he was going to say next.

"Unfortunately, for all the usefulness of human buildings, humans hunt spiders, although they don't actually seem to prey on us. These lumbering creatures have been seen to kill spiders for sport, slamming their paws down on a spider just because it was walking in the human's line of sight. If you see them, run to a place of cover.

"Similarly, while they can spot spiders quickly and easily, they almost seem oblivious to our webs. If you build one in their pathway, they will walk through the web, which will cling to them but even a Darwin's Bark Spider won't stop a human."

Click. Even without looking, Boris knew it was Billy and knew what the question was. He didn't look, just answered.

"No, Billy, Shelob wasn't a real spider, she was a myth parents made up to encourage their spiderlings to try to achieve anything."

A series of buzzes emanated from the machine. One by one all eighteen of the spiderlings dropped from the system.

Boris took a look at the clock on the computer. He still had significant time left in the webinar, possibly even enough to cover all the topics, if the students could rejoin and Billy didn't interrupt with his inane comments. It wasn't that Billy was not intelligent, although he wasn't particularly brilliant. His problem was that he was immature for his age. There was a chance, perhaps a slim chance, that he would actually take something away from the series of webinars. If so, he would probably get more out of them than Charlotte. She was bright and really wasn't learning anything she didn't already know. The best Boris could do with her was reinforce what her parents had taught her. Despite that, he would much rather interact with Charlotte during the sessions than with Billy.

The chimes began and spiderlings started to show up in the guest list again. Four, eight, twelve…the chimes stopped with thirteen. The other five probably figured the webinar was effectively over and they had gained ten minutes of their lives back. He hoped they would use the time productively.

Boris was surprised to see that Billy was one of the returning spiderlings.

"Welcome back, everyone. Since we only have a few minutes left, I'm going to take everyone off mute from my end and let you ask questions. If you aren't actually asking a question, please keep the computer muted from your end."

"Professor Boris, given what you were saying before we got dropped, is it better to spin a web near humans or avoid them altogether?" Betsy asked.

"It is really a judgment call. I would probably suggest…"

"Mom, could you bring me something to eat? Boris's webinar is running long."

"I'm sorry, whoever that is, could you please mute your computer?"

"Here you are. It's only a midge. I don't want you to ruin your appetite."

"Thanks, Mom."

"Please mute your computer." Boris paused and didn't hear anything. "Thank you. As I was saying, I would probably suggest that at your age you stay away from....Whoever is chewing into their microphone, could you please stop? It is really rather disgusting sounding."

The noise continued, followed by a loud belch. Boris could hear a couple of the other spiderlings who hadn't muted their computers laughing. He punched the mute button on his computer to silence all of them.

Breathe. Focus.

"At your age, I would recommend staying away from humans while you really learn not only the basics of web spinning, but become very proficient in it. Once you are comfortable with building your web, should you decide to relocate it, you can consider moving it near a human building."

Boris paused and was greeted with silence. No further quest...

"I'm sorry. I've muted all of you again. If you have a question, please send it using the text box and I'll answer you."

Click. A question from Mina.

"It's really a matter of trial and error. You build a web using your best judgment and if it works, you could be set for life. Otherwise, you abandon the web and try again. My first web was built too close to the web of another spider. That spider had built a better location, in the path of many insects. I watched as it got fat feasting on plump flies while I was starving on the occasional gnat. Even so, it didn't occur to me to move my web until I spoke with an older, more experienced spider. These webinars are available to allow you to learn from my mistakes and not wait so long to make a correction when necessary.

"Are there any other questions? Remember, you're muted, so send them in via the chat box."

Nothing came in.

"Ok, then I have a little homework assignment for you."

Boris could practically hear the groans and expected that Billy was rolling at least six of his eyes.

Click. Naturally.

"No, doing the homework isn't a requirement. You aren't being graded on these webinars. They are for informational purposes so you'll be able to live a long and satisfying life. You don't have to attend them, you don't have to listen to them, you don't have to do what I'm about to suggest. But if you do, I can almost guarantee that your first webs will be more successful than mine was.

"What I want you to do is go out and pick a spot that you think would make a good location for a web. Don't put out any silk. Just imagine where you would anchor your web. Feel the wind and guess where the bridge will connect. Picture the resulting web with you standing in one corner of it and then wait. While you wait, pay attention to any insects that are in the area. Are they flying near where your imaginary web is? Is there a place nearby where a web could be built that is getting more insect traffic that would have been a better place to build your web?

"Try this thought experiment in a couple different places."

Click.

"No, Charlotte, as I said before, it isn't an assignment. I won't ask about it at next week's webinar. If anyone wants to discuss it with me off line, you all have my web address. Whatever we discuss about this homework will remain between each of you and me if you choose to share it.

"Are there any final questions?"

Boris waited a few moments without any clicks sounding. The system showed that all thirteen spiderlings were still logged in, although they didn't necessarily mean any of them were still paying attention. He glanced down the list and made a guess at which ones had scuttled away immediately after logging back in, but at least they had logged back in.

"Thanks for joining me. I hope you all found it a useful session. Please consider the 'homework' I gave you. Next week's webinar will be on how to handle and prepare the insects you catch: Web hosting."

Sons of the Spider

By Toni Johnson

Toni Johnson is an illustrator as well as an author of science fiction and fantasy. She lives deep in a forest in Chicagoland with her husband and daughter, having grand adventures with imaginary monsters. To see more of her work, please visit her blog at www.tonij.com.

The clouds finally part, letting rays of moonlight down to the forest floor. I race through the underbrush, arms up to protect my face from branches. The woods look like they will thin out ahead. I can't hear the creatures chasing me anymore, but I don't slow down, not even as my lungs feel about to burst and my legs burn with exhaustion.

The forest opens to a narrow road. I feel the gravel, hear it crunch beneath my hiking boots. I pause, just for a second. I need to find help. But the road winds out of sight in either direction. A distant shriek sends a chill through my heart. I pick a direction, and start running again.

Not far along the service road, I see a sign. The park ranger's cabin lies ahead. I let out a relieved breath; I picked the right way. I can get help there. I will tell the ranger everything about what I found lurking in these woods.

Tears fill my eyes as I run. What if the ranger doesn't believe me? What if nobody is home? What if those things catch me before I can enlist the ranger's help? I swallow back my doubts, and press on. The monsters frighten me, but I'm even more afraid of what will happen if they spread from the park to where people live. For my family, and everyone's families, I have to try.

A laugh bubbles up when I see the cabin. I will my legs to run up the driveway, past the ranger's pickup truck, and up the steps. I pound on the thick wooden door.

I shout for someone, anyone, to come to the door.

There is no answer.

But I see light behind the curtains, and smoke drifts up from the chimney; the park ranger must be inside. I have no more energy to run back to town if not, so I keep slamming my fists against the wood. From the corner of my eye, I think I see movement inside.

The door swings open. Finally! The ranger fills the open doorway, buttoning up his tan overshirt. He stares down at me with eyes shaded beneath the brim of his hat.

All of my words rush out at once.

"I saw something terrible! In the woods. Please, help!"

He looks past me, as if searching for the creatures that chased me this far. His lips form a deep frown. I hear the faint, monstrous scream again. I beg the man again for help. With a grunt of frustration, he pulls me inside the cabin. It is warm inside, and the comforting glow from the lamps and fireplace almost put me at ease. Almost. Nothing will erase the horror of I saw out there.

The park ranger all but pushes me down into the chair across from his desk. He tugs his hat low, but I can see it on his face. He thinks I'm wasting his time. I'm not. I know what I saw, and everyone is in danger.

He takes a cold cup of coffee from his side of the desk and shoves it into my hands. Then he settles into his own chair. He folds his arms and leans back.

"You say you saw something in the woods."

"Yes. Monsters."

He glares. I feel the heat of it. The hatred.

"I was woken up for this? Do you have any proof to back up this story?"

I pull an egg fragment out of my pocket. The slimy interior glows green. The outer shell is black with swirling designs. It almost looks like writing. I place it on his desk.

He doesn't look at it. He doesn't want it to be real. Just like I didn't want it to be real.

"Why don't you tell me what you think you saw? From the beginning?"

Thinking about it makes my stomach turn. I want to scream, to hide, but the world has to be warned.

"I was on the backcountry trails. There was a full moon, as you know, so I planned to hike through 'til morning. But I lost the light when the clouds rolled in. Then I lost the trail. There was a glow in the distance, and I thought I had found campers. I didn't notice the webs until it was too late."

I pause to take a sip of the coffee. Just long enough to make sure the park ranger is listening.

"The glow was not from a campfire, but from eggs bigger than a trash can. They coated the ground as far as I could see. Hundreds, maybe thousands of egg sacks glowing an unearthly green. I shined my flashlight into the trees. Webs hung between the branches like a fog. I tried to avoid touching any of it. I turned to leave the way I'd come. But my foot grazed one of those horrid eggs. My pant leg stuck for a moment. The egg sack trembled, mocked my attempt to escape. The webs above my head danced. That was when I heard it. A malicious scream, followed by mandibles clacking."

The park ranger glowers at me. I know how it must sound. Monsters in the woods? He must think I'm crazy.

I feel sweat beading on my forehead.

"Please, you have to believe me. Everything I say is true!"

He slides a map across the desk to me. He tosses a red marker on top.

"Can you at least tell me where you say these 'eggs' are located?"

"Here. I think. But, they're gone now." I circle a section of the park. "I saw the spider that laid those eggs. As big as your truck out front, with eyes like torches. It was laughing. It jabbed at me. I managed to roll away. I even used a large branch to hit its face. Poked out two eyes."

The park ranger slams his fist onto the desk.

"How dare you!" He sees my confusion and fear. He corrects his sentence. "How dare you waste my time. Those cuts on your arms and face are probably from running through brambles."

"No! See this scratch? It is still glowing. Her venom paralyzed my arm. I only just got movement back. We fought for several long minutes. I narrowly escaped. I ran, but I couldn't see the moon or stars. My maps were lost in the fight, as was my flashlight. I went deeper into the field of eggs. The farther I went, the brighter they glowed. Until..." I can't help but shudder. "That noise. The spider's scream pierced my mind. It was an incantation. I doubled over, sick. Then there was a sound like an earthquake. The eggs were hatching. But it was not a spider army that emerged, but monsters that looked like men. Those glowing eyes, too many to truly be human."

The park ranger tenses.

"Did you get a good look at these men?"

I feel so useless. I shake my head.

"It was too dark. The green glow died back when the spider's sons were born. They came at me, and I ran. I didn't stop until I reached the service road. I followed that back here. Please. You have to believe me. Call for help. Burn the entire park if you have to. Do it before the spider and her sons make their move."

The park ranger rubs his chin in silence.

Maybe he doesn't want to believe me, but he needs to. I can't fight those things. Not alone.

A moment later, he stands up and beckons me.

"Follow me. We should... use my phone to call for help. It's in the back room."

I straighten up. No words could be sweeter right now. He does believe me!

"Thank you. Thank you so much. I'm so glad I found your cabin. Now we can stop these monsters before they strike."

He leads me away from the main room through a side door. I take a sip of my coffee. The back room is cold and dark. The ranger flicks the light switch on. There is a single desk here, unmanned, with a chunky black landline phone to one side. The park ranger points to a chair, and I sit.

He closes the door behind us, and I hear the lock click. The sound makes me grip my cup tighter. With creatures so large, no simple lock will be enough.

Something about this room is off. There is a smell. When we walked in, I thought I was remembering the putrid spider eggs, but this is different. Coppery and sickening. I hesitate to look down, and gag at what I see there.

Blood on the rug.

A severed arm pokes out from beneath the desk.

I need to run.

I leap from the chair, but a heavy hand lands on my shoulder. I feel something pierce my skin, and everything goes numb on that side. I turn. The park ranger removes his hat, revealing two more pairs of eyes above the first. All six begin to burn with green fire.

He smiles, and his teeth are sharp.

END

Anansi and Brother Death,

...or Why Spider's Webs Are Found On The Ceiling

by Michael Auld

Michael Auld grew up hearing Anansi stories in Kingston, Jamaica. As a student at Howard University he illustrated his version of the story "Anansi and the Yam Hills". For 30 years he taught storytelling, illustration and cartooning to adults and children. He and his wife live in Washington, D.C.. His work can be viewed at www.anansistories.com

Once in a before time, Anansi was walking far into the bush. Soon he came to a house with a very, very, VERY old man sitting inside the mouth of the front door. The old man looked like skin and dry bones. Anansi gathered up his courage and said.

"Good day sir! I have been walking all morning and would love to have a cool drink of ice water."

However, the old man said nothing.

Anansi, who thought that the old man might have been deaf, walked closer to the seated figure and repeated in a loud voice.

"I said... GOOD MORNING SIR! MAY I HAVE A DRINK OF WATER?"

Nevertheless, the old man said nothing. Anansi scratched his head and said, "Oh, you said to go inside the house and help myself?"

The old man still said nothing to Anansi. Anansi walked past the old man and went into his house and not only helped himself to ice cold water but to as much food as he could eat. When he had finished eating, Anansi went outside to see the old man who was sitting in the same spot by the door. Anansi thanked him for his hospitality and returned home.

The next day Anansi went to the house of the old man and again ate his fill. Still, the old man said nothing to Anansi.

On the third day, Anansi the spider brought his eldest daughter to the old man's house.

"Good morning sir," Anansi greeted. "Since you have been so kind to me I have brought my beautiful daughter who wants to be a cook. I will give her to you as your wife," said Anansi. Then he turned to his daughter. "Here is a wedding ring. Now go into the house and fix your father a nice plate of food."

The old man still said nothing.

The next day Anansi got up early. He headed for the old man's house. The old man had not moved and was still sitting by his door. Anansi said his good morning and entered the house. He called for his daughter but she did not answer. He knew that she liked Hide-and-Seek so he looked in every closet. He then checked under the bed. Although he knew that it was a dangerous hiding place, he looked into the icebox, but he could not find her. Anansi searched all over the house but he was not able to find his daughter.

He thought of one place that he had not looked.

"I know where she is. She is hiding in the oven!" he said as he opened the door to the stove's oven. Anansi jumped back. For in the oven lay his daughter's wedding ring. Anansi rushed outside the house and grabbed the old man by the collar.

"Where is my daughter?" he shouted.

Finally, the old man spoke in a deep raspy voice. "Do… you …know… who… I… am?" He said slowly, chewing on every word that escaped his throat.

"Yes." Anansi said. "You are my son-in-law."

"Hah! Your son-in-law!" The old man rasped. "My name is Death and you came looking for me. I did not invite you into my house. To add insult to injury, you brought me your ugly daughter… so I ate her. Now I am going to have you for lunch," Brother Death said as he grabbed Anansi by the shirt.

Anansi tore the buttons from his shirt, slipped out of it and ran for his life. He ran as fast as he could in the belief that he could easily outdistance an old man like Brother Death. However, wherever Anansi turned, Death was right behind him. Finally, out of desperation, Anansi lunged for a tree limb and climbed as high as he could. To his surprise, Brother Death did not follow Anansi up the tree. Death could not climb!

Brother Death picked up a rock, an old shoe, anything that he could find, and threw them at Anansi. They all missed. Death could not throw either. He soon ran out of things to throw. Therefore, he ran around under the tree in search of any missile. Once when he took his eyes off Anansi, the frightened spider jumped off the tree and bolted for his home.

As he neared his house Anansi shouted out to his wife.

"Aso! Grab the children and climb up into the ceiling! Death is after me!"

"What did you say, Anansi?" His wife asked.

"I SAID... GRAB THE CHILDREN AND CLIMB UP TO THE CEILING!" Anansi cried.

"You said do what with the potato peelings?" his wife asked.

"I said... Oh, Never mind!" Anansi cried in frustration.

He quickly rushed into his house, grabbed his wife and children, and climbed up into the ceiling with them.

"Grab hold of a wooden beam and hold on tight!" He shouted.

As Brother Death rushed in the door, Anansi and his family were safely clinging to a beam in the ceiling. Brother Death calmly picked up a burlap bag, pulled up a chair, sat down under the dangling spider family and crossed his legs.

Half an hour passed and Anansi's youngest son said to his father,"Oh, Puppa, my hands are hurting me. I can't hold on any longer."

"Hold on son, for if you fall Death is going to get you," Anansi said to his child. However, the boy could not hold on any longer. Therefore, he fell.

Death caught the boy and opened the burlap bag. "It is your father I want... not you." Then he placed the child into the burlap bag.

Soon, another of Anansi's daughters cried out to her father. "Puppa, please...my hands are tired. I am going to fall".

"Fall and Death is going to get you!" Anansi answered.

His daughter fell and Death placed her in the burlap bag with her brother.

"I don't want you. I want your father," said Death.

Soon Anansi's other daughter and son fell. So did his wife, Aso. Finally, Anansi's own hands became tired. First, the left hand froze and lost its grip. However, Anansi held on tight with only his right hand. He exercised the frozen left hand in the hope of using it to relieve the right hand. Anansi's mind began to race.

"Brother Death." He called. "I am so fat from eating all your food that if I fall I will just splatter into pieces. There will not be enough of me left to put in that bag. You will only have enough meat to make spider-burgers. However, if you go into the kitchen you will find a barrel of flour. Get the barrel and set it under me so that the flour will cushion the fall. I won't splatter. I will just be battered."

"Mmmhh..." Death exhaled, rubbed his chin and smiled, showing all his 37-and-a-half teeth. "Kentucky

Fried Spider for dinner, heh? Or, maybe I can make delicious, spicy Jerk Spider from Anansi and his family!"

Anansi figured that the flour barrel was so heavy that it would take four men to lift it. This would give him time to escape. As Brother Death went into the kitchen Anansi was about to let go and drop from the ceiling. However, in a flash Death was back under Anansi with the flour barrel. Anansi had underestimated Brother Death's strength. As Brother Death wobbled the barrel from side to side, he bent over the barrel to make sure that it was exactly under Anansi. The cunning spider dropped on top of the old man's head, dunking his face into the flour. The flour bath temporarily blinded Death.

Anansi jumped off Death's head, released his family and they ran for their lives. Death has never caught Anansi the Spider. That is why there are Anansi Stories to this day. When you see spider webs on the ceiling it belongs to Anansi. He is still trying to get away from Death.

The Entomologist's Discovery

By Wren Roberts

Wren lives outside of Chicago with three naughty kittens and her partner. When not knitting or trying to learn Russian, she spends probably way too much time watching old, cancelled sci-fi shows. By way of a day job, she works with children with emotional and behavioral needs.

Wren can be found on twitter as @gardsmyg. She also sporadically maintains her personal blog at www.wrenroberts.com, where she muses about knitting, writing, and not posting in her blog enough. Primarily that last one.

There was no whistle of the kettle to wake Slawek in the morning. It wasn't something that immediately registered as unusual, but as his eyes adjusted to wakefulness and he saw a morning mist outside the window of his small room, he realized something wasn't quite right.

Katharine was always the first one up. Katharine always put the kettle on. Katharine always made tea.

The wood of the floor was smooth under foot. The cot creaked as he stood up. He pulled on yesterday's t-shirt, ignoring the smear of blood at the hem, as he opened the door and stepped into the short hallway. If he turned to his right, he'd find Davis's and Katharine's bedrooms. He didn't want to think about Davis just yet. He turned left to go into the combined living space of their research cabin.

The kettle was on the stove. He picked it up, the water sloshing inside. Mostly empty, and not even warm. He checked the propane tank. Half full, still. He frowned.

Yesterday, Katharine had put his tea in his blue Thermos. He'd taken the tea with him in the Jeep as he'd gone out to meet up with Davis. The tea had remained undrunk.

No, he wasn't going to think about that yet.

He had a dilemma, though. The water supply was outside. But going outside would mean confronting yesterday's truth. There wasn't enough water left in the kettle worth heating. He'd skip the tea. Not ideal, but necessary.

He went straight to the small research lab that occupied a small bedroom at the end of the cabin. He checked all the mesh cages that held the team's live samples. Katharine had collected several Lepidoptera species, including some really lovely Ornithoptera chimaera. Their green butterfly wings matched almost perfectly Slawek's own Rhombodera papuana sample. His mantises were also thriving, in part because he'd only collected females. After this inspection, it was time to check on the pride and joy of Davis's research--the spiders. Several occupied beautiful orb webs in their own mesh boxes. The recent Selenocosmia capture was still working on the bird they had fed it a few days back. It was starting to smell, but there was no way Slawek was going to stick his hand in there with that thing.

When Davis had first captured it, they had hoped it was the spider they were looking for, but the locals had denied it was the Bulora Mapoo of legend. They had a different name for the terrifyingly large spider. It'd been the biggest disappointment in the eight months since they'd arrived in New Guinea. When they had observed its web, it became clear it wasn't the spider they were looking for. They had four months left on their grant and despite discovering several previously unidentified insects, the Bulora Mapoo, the Widower Twin, had eluded them.

The Selenocosmia began growling, which was Slawek's cue to move away. It hadn't gotten out of its enclosure yet, but it also hadn't tried. He wasn't going to wrestle with that thing when it was mad, especially not alone.

He wondered where Katharine had gone. He'd gone to bed while Katharine was still speaking with the tribal widows. They had been arguing about what to do with Davis. Which had happened after the stand-off with the tribal elders, who had wanted to burn the Jeep and Davis together.

They were all afraid of the spider. It was what had inspired Davis to come here. Local legends of the fearsome man-eating spider had inspired his imagination. Davis had wanted to find it, dispell the stories, and become famous in the process. Slawek had been his research assistant for almost three years. Davis was definitely chasing the elusive tenure track more than he was chasing the mythic spider.

Not that Davis would ever get tenure now.

Slawek shivered. He'd thrown up yesterday morning when he'd found Davis. His colleague had been face down, sprawled out among the underbrush of the jungle. Far enough from the village to have died silently, but close enough to make everyone uneasy. Something had stripped the flesh from his arm. It wasn't clear if he'd already been dead or if that'd been what killed him.

Umina, the local village brat who followed them like a lost puppy, had followed him. It'd been her poking at Davis's body that had made the bile of his stomach churn.

"Found it," she had whispered. She had motioned for him to come closer, but the white of the bone and the fleshy bits that clung to it wouldn't let him. The meat of his arm had been torn asunder, as if something had snaked up his arm, biting all the way. The girl had poked her finger at the bone, which is what had made Slawek's stomach finally give. At least she had the courtesy to pretend she didn't hear him wretching into the scrub.

He'd forgotten about the tea. The last of the water in his canteen hadn't done him much as far as clearing his mouth, but it was better than nothing. By the time he had clipped it back to his belt, he realized the girl was doing a bit more than poking at the old man's bones.

"Hey!" He barked. She didn't flinch and continued sticking her hands in his various pockets. She was already wearing his glasses, his watch flopping around her wrist. From his breast pocket she relieved him of a lighter and some cigarettes. It was this indignity that urged him to take a few steps closer. "What are you doing?"

She looked back at him and snorted. "Doc is dead. He don't need stuff." She started untying his boots.

"Stop that! We don't even know what killed him!"

Slawek really didn't want to get any closer, but if this stupid girl didn't stop, he wouldn't have a choice.

She saved him the trouble. Umina got right up and walked up to him. She was a full head shorter than him, and she looked really silly in the old man's glasses, but she could make a face as intimidating as any of her warrior brothers.

"You want stay here? Find out? I tell you what kill him. But you, like Doc, won't believe. Even when you know."

Slawek shook himself from that terrible memory. He didn't want to think about wrestling Davis's body into the Jeep by himself because the girl refused to help. He didn't want to think of the argument among the village elders when they'd driven back into town. He didn't want to think about the penis-wagging it had caused, or that the Jeep had almost been burned with torches.

It was a shame, however, that an anthropoligist hadn't been a part of their team. Even Slawek recognized all the weird shit that he'd witnessed was an ethnographic gold mine. But they weren't here for tribal relations, or studying blood feuds, or any of that. They were here for the spider.

The spider, folklore said, had been a dangerous, poisonous creature. One day, a clever and fast man had cleaved the spider in two. But rather than die, the two halves of the spider had regrown and turned into the widower twin, Bulora mapoo. A single spider inhabited two bodies, and they hunted in pairs. And of course they were magic. That much was a given. It was folklore, after all. One half had the power to hypnotize and keep a victim easy prey for the other half's venomous bite. However, for as long as you looked at the non-hypnotic half, the spider could not destroy you. The terror came from never knowing which half of the spider you were looking at.

Davis had a theory, and it was one both Slawek and Katharine had agreed made sense. In a land where a single blood feud could wipe out two tribes in a year, having a spider to blame for a death meant there was nothing to avenge. Murder could become a tragic accident rather than a cyclical destruction. In a jungle where bird-eating spiders had the bite to kill children, it was easy to imagine one that could kill a man.

The locals were insistent that Davis had been killed by a widower twin. The elders had been incensed that he had brought a victim back into the village. That was another catch. The spiders went with their victims, so to bring a body into the village was to bring doom to everyone. Never mind that Slawek had noted no usual spiders when hoisting up Davis's body. Of course there had been spiders--there were always spiders, it was statistically impossible for there to not be spiders--but there was no way a spider had killed Davis. The wounds were too large. It'd probably been a large cat of some sort. And that certainly hadn't come with them in the Jeep.

It was time, he decided, to look for Katharine. Look for Katharine and face the truth of Davis's body, which was likely still on the front porch of the research cabin. It'd been where the village widows had brought it after rescuing the Jeep from being burned. Katharine was probably with the widows. They would need to decide together how to proceed with Davis and his death. This also might be the end of their grant, but that was another thing

Slawek opened the door and stumbled back. A ginormous web had been woven across the doorway. Hanging in the middle, upside down, a female golden orb weaver the size of his head stared back at him. He instantly felt stupid for being startled. Orb weavers had been building across doorways and windows since mankind had moved indoors. They were a common spider, and he was an entomologist, damn it. Spiders weren't meant to scare him. Especially not one so harmless. Especially not Nephila pilipes. They had been the original spiders that had drawn him into this career path.

He crawled under the web and into the morning mist that still clung to the jungle. Unnamed villages like the one they were based out of weren't like the villages of Slawek's Poland. Here, the huts and cabins were far-flung, maybe four or five clustered near each other, but still barely neighbors. It could take up to ten minutes to get to another satellite of tribal homes. The village was merely the territory the tribe claimed as theirs. The research cabin was nearest to the center as it could get. But even still, they basically lived in the jungle, and the mist this morning was thick and made this portion feel like it was a world of its own.

Davis's boots were carefully placed near the stairs of the porch. However, his body was nowhere to be found. Slawek swallowed. Perhaps the widows had convinced Katharine to remove the body away from the hut cluster and into the true jungle. The jungle where you could get lost. Or killed.

He looked back at the orb weaver and considered his bare feet. Not wanting to disturb her, he thought about putting Davis's boots on, but they were each filled with a fine mesh of spider-silk webbing. Even knocking the boots several times did not elicit a spider, or even the hint of a spider or even an egg sac. He decided to explore the boots and their webs more thoroughly later. Maybe this would be his first true discovery, and he could name it after Davis. But first he had to find Katharine and figure out what they were going to do.

Slawek jumped off the porch and headed in the direction of the widows' hut. Once a woman's husband died, she lived a somewhat secluded life on the edge of the village. She would never speak to another man again, and would begin speaking the secret language that only widows knew. They would still speak the standard tongue, and even English at times, but never to another man. Not their sons, not their brothers. Not even a foreigner such a Slawek.

It had been the unusual presence of the widows that had stopped the village elders from burning the Jeep last night. It was strange for the widows to venture too far from their hut, let alone to stare down the ranking men of their tribe. Their silence carried more power than their voices ever had before their husbands died.

It felt more like swimming than walking, Slawek decided, as he made his way. The bare feet ended up being a blessing, being able to feel his way along a path he could barely see. He'd tread this trail many times before. Dinner with the widows had been one of Katharine's favorite ways to spend an evening. He and Davis had accompanied for the pure strangeness of it all.

Usually men could not enter the widows' hut. Their status as foreigners had allowed a little indiscretion, even if that wall of silence had remained intact. Katharine enjoyed her privilege status in that hut, and frequently teased them about how powerless they were there. Davis liked to remind Slawek that this was because Katharine was the most junior member of the team. Slawek shivered. He was the most senior member now.

His foot hit something round and slippery. Somehow he just knew he didn't want to look, but he had to look. He looked down an instantly regretted it. Bone. From the size, probably a tibia. Why the fuck was there a bone out here?

He took a deep breath and calmed himself. It was probably from dinner. It wasn't human. It couldn't be human. He was just shook up from yesterday. The yesterday he still didn't fully want to think about, and if he wasn't careful, would think about. It was from a pig. They'd had pork not too long ago, hadn't they?

He didn't think about the small bits of flesh that still clung to it in places.

It was from a pig. A pig.

He started walking more quickly up the path. He hated this fog. He hated not seeing where he was going, or what was in front of him for that matter. The jungle was bullshit. The bugs were bullshit. He'd be glad when he was finally back in the lab at their dumpy second-rate university.

Slawek practically tripped over the low gate outside the hut. It cut him right in the balls, and his body pitched forward. Hands flailing, he grabbed onto anything that he could find. He let out a small yelp as some metal wire keeping the fence together cut through his palm. When he looked at it, it seemed like both too little and too much blood from the wound. He considered his tetanus shot, then balled his hand into a fist.

He took a deep breath. There'd be cloth inside he could wrap around his hand. Something to sop up the blood tricking down his wrist.

He scrambled up the few steps onto the porch. Out of the corner of his eye, he saw a set of feet laying in the corner. He didn't let his gaze linger. He just pushed open the door and kicked it shut behind him.

"Slawek?" Katharine whisper-shrieked.

It was dark and his eyes hadn't yet adjusted. The windows still had the shutters shuttered, casting the hut into an unhelpful dimness. He looked around for his colleague, but all he could see was shadows.

"Katharine, what's wrong?" The moment of silence which followed seemed to stretch out into seconds. "Katharine! What is it?"

"It's in here."

"What?" As his eyes began adjusting, he recognized the large rectangular devoid of almost any furniture. Just a few cots pushed against the wall. Cots that were filled with the shapes of women. He started shuffling in the direction of her voice.

"Shh. They're both here."

"I don't—"

"They're all dead." There was Katharine, wedged between a cot and the wall. That's all he could let himself see.

"We need to talk about Davis."

Katharine looked up at him. "We need to get out of here."

In the very back of his ears, Slawek heard something plop onto the wooden floor. It was a strange sound. Like it was too loud, even though he could barely hear it. After which, there was nothing more to be heard.

"We need to get out of here," she repeated. "It's here."

He bit his lip. "Katharine, what are you—"

"The bulora mapoo. I don't know which one is which. I thought I had it, but I blinked and it was gone and now they're hiding."

Slawek took a moment to consider what his colleague was telling him. The damn spider they'd been hunting was in the hut. But instead of capturing it, Katharine wanted them to leave. Then he remembered she'd said all the widows were dead. But who was to say they weren't just sleeping and Katharine wasn't being hysterical?

He offered a hand to her, which she gladly took. She slid out from behind the cot.

"We should get one as a sample."

Katharine shook her head, scanning for something over his shoulder. "Some things just aren't supposed to be sampled." She stepped around him and glued her back to his. "And I'm getting out of here alive."

Definitely hysterical, Slawek decided. But he would humor her. Together, they started shuffling towards the door. Halfway there, he spotted the arachnid he'd spent so many years thinking about.

It was bigger than he though, even for Papua New Guinea. Its leg span made it a little larger than his hand. A green triangle on his back appeared shiny, even in the darkness of the hut. It just sat on the floor, staring at him.

How was this supposed to work? As long as you looked at the right one, you were safe from it and its partner. But if you were looking at the wrong one, you'd find yourself paralyzed. Ripe pickings for the right spider. That's what made the creature so fascinating: you never knew which spider you were looking at.

Slawek wondered which spider this was. What a funny idea. He'd help Katharine get out, and then they could get their traps from the research cottage, and then he could come back, trap it, and name it after Davis. It was a perfect plan.

Katharine's back peeled off of his. She was still walking. He heard her footsteps continue, pause, and then run out the door.

He would follow her. Just as soon as he was finished admiring the elusive spider. There wasn't anything like seeing a beautiful new species for the first time.

This was the right spider. Even if there was something to those folktales, he was looking at the right spider, so he was safe. He was certain of it. Even as he felt soft legs climbing on his calf. This was the right spider.

The bite hurt. A lot. The pain seared its way through his nervous system and turned his vision to white. He didn't even know he was falling until his head slammed into the floor. Just before he lost consciousness, he felt the flesh being torn from his leg.

It was the right spider. Just the wrong one for him.

Taste Test

By Joshua Byrd

Joshua lives "on the edge of farm country" southwest of Chicago. He enjoys steampunk crafting and cosplay. A novice ventriloquist, he and his companion Bosik provide smiles and laughter for their friends and family.

The trembling strands of her web woke Nnenia from her nap. These were not the frantic thrashings of prey trying to escape, but the steady, even tread of Chepri the Beetle King. When he saw that she was awake, he turned and crept down the trunk of the tree to which she'd anchored her web. When he reached the ground he resumed his human form, that of a youth on the cusp of manhood.

Long-limbed and leanly muscled he wore a knee-length linen kilt in the fashion of the Narmerite people of the Northeast. Hammered copper bands gleamed bright against the mahogany skin of his upper arms. His thick hair hung in numerous waxed braids. Among the many elaborately beaded necklaces he wore was a simple obsidian amulet with an amber inlay in the shape of a beetle.

Nnenia secured a tether line to her web and lowered herself to the ground. There she, too, resumed human form. Her flesh sagged over her bones, and the once brilliant green and yellow colors of her caftan had long since faded into bland shades of brown. Her feet were bare, the skin cracked and tough. She had shaved off her hair years ago, but her scalp was covered with coarse, white fuzz like a man's beard. Her only ornament was an obsidian amulet with an amber inlay in the shape of a spider.

Chepri bowed with deep respect. Before his parents had been born, Nnenia had ascended to become the Spider Queen. After the death of her husband she had chosen to retire to the forest, returning to visit her family once a year. She had seen her home grow from a village, to a town, and finally a city. Her grandchildren were now having grandchildren of their own.

"My sister queen," Chepri said in a voice not yet fully deepened, "I have come to bring you to council."

He held out his hands and Nnenia placed her fingertips in the cup they formed, resuming her spider shape. Chepri lifted her to his shoulder and she made herself comfortable in his hair.

To insure that their progeny would remain close to Nature, the First Ones Adjatay and Jazhara had each chosen twelve animals and bonded their spirits to the souls of their sons and daughters setting them apart as royalty with the Lion King and Elephant Queen to rule over them all.

For two dozen generations the Totem Council had reigned over the people of Ifriqah in relative peace and prosperity. Then came the ships waving the banner of the crescent swords crossed beneath a six-pointed star carrying the warriors and priests of the Faith in the One True God.

The armies of the Faithful had swept across the northern coast. Undeterred by the Arasha Desert, they had marched south crushing all resistance beneath their heels.

With them came engineers, scholars, doctors, and merchants who built roads, bridges, libraries and clinics. The old Totemist shrines were demolished to make way for the temples of the True Faith. What few that survived had fallen into ruins.

For this meeting the Council was gathering at the southern edge of the lava lake at the summit of a volcano. The war-priest who would rise to become Qalif of Seba had proclaimed it a portal to Hell and forbade all to climb its slopes. In Nnenia's opinion he need not have bothered. Even if humans could withstand the oppressive heat, the poisons in the air would kill them in minutes. However nothing in Nature could harm the Totem Royals. Here they could speak freely without fear of human interference.

Nnenia crept down Chepri's neck and arm to his hand. He carried her to a boulder and she crawled off his flesh onto the stone resuming her human form. The others gathered assuming their places in two half circles, men to the north, women to the south. Finally Obareth the Lion King and Zhenga the Elephant Queen came from the east and west respectively completing the Council circle.

Subira the Ant Queen spoke first. "Prince Ozer has come of age and returned to the palace."

Nnenia was dismayed. Had it really been that long? As the Spider Queen she had the power to judge a human heart by tasting the blood that passed through it. She grimaced as she recalled her last visit to the palace. The Bade-shah's blood had been sweet, cloyingly so and Nnenia had feared her palate had been ruined.

After the conquest, mapmakers had divided Ifriqah into kingdoms and imirates which the Aga-shah, Imir of the Holy City and Supreme Qalif of the True Faith, doled out as prizes to his generals according to their accomplishments. Qinyah, one of the richest realms had gone to the Aga-shah's son-in-law.

When the armies of the Faithful had swept over the continent the Totem Royal Council had gone into hiding rather than try and lead their people in any kind of active resistance. After all, the Elephant Queen had reminded them, human empires rose and fell like the waves of the sea. It was the land itself and the people who mattered. Nnenia smiled as she imagined the reactions of the various imirs, qalifs, and bade-shahs if they ever learned that they ruled at the sufferance of the Council.

Twenty years ago Nnenia had passed judgment on the newly ascended bade-shah of Qinyah. As a thirdborn son, he had been destined for a life of scholarship and had rather resented having to leave the Great Library and take his father's throne. However the execution of his middle brother for the murders of his father and elder brother had left him little choice.

He was not stupid, but not as brilliant as he thought himself, Nnenia had reported to the Council. They had agreed that intellectual vanity was an acceptable flaw. The Serpent Queen had used her powers of persuasion to have the Ant Queen's husband named Grand Vizier. Together they managed the kingdom while the Bade-shah studied obscure scrolls and debated philosophy with his favorite medji.

However, despite having taken the requisite four wives, the Bade-shah had sired only six children, all of them girls. It had seemed he would have to choose his successor from among his sons-in-law when the sudden demise of his first wife had created a vacancy in the court. That vacancy had been filled by none other than the Aga-shah's youngest daughter. Within a year of her arrival the new queen had given birth to a son. Now that son was about to celebrate his coming of age.

Little was known about the prince since he had been raised in seclusion by a household of priests personally selected by his grandfather.

"What is he like?" Zhenga the Elephant Queen asked.

Subira shrugged. "I only saw him at the welcome ceremony. He made a great display of piety, but whether it was genuine or not, I cannot say. Only our sister queen Nnenia can determine if he is worthy to rule."

Nnenia sighed. She longed to be back at home on the edge of the jungle awaiting her successor. Most of the peoples of Ifriqah tended to embrace a common Totem. The Narmerites for example nearly always identified with the Beetle. In fact Narmer had been the first Beetle King. However heritage was no guarantee of affinity, and in the cities especially there was a mix of Totems represented.

Of course one of the first things the qalifs had done was to outlaw the ceremony that revealed people's personal Totems. Yet the divine magic of Adjatay and Jazhara was strong enough to ensure that, short of slaughtering the entire population of Ifriqah, the Council would never be broken. When Nnenia's life-thread had run its course, her amulet would find its way to her successor and form a bond. A new Spider Queen would ascend after feasting on the flesh of the old.

"Then it shall be so," Zhenga declared. "Nnenia will return with Subira and pass judgment on the prince."

Zhenga had reminded Nnenia that she had only a brief span of time to carry out her judgment. The prince was scheduled to undergo a ritual in which he would be formally anointed as his father's heir. Something about that ceremony rendered its participants immune from Nnenia's powers. More to the point, her fangs wouldn't pierce their skin.

The Council had learned that the hard way. One of Nnenia's predecessors had been too late in judging

Kaysar III of Abunia. He had begun his reign by poisoning the air in the harem killing his father's 4 wives and 20 concubines, his 3 younger sisters, 31 handmaidens, and 42 eunuchs. Scholars were divided as to whether his cruelty had been rooted in some form of madness.

His reign had been mercifully short. Among the gifts of state sent by the Bade-shah of Qango had been a silverback gorilla. This animal had broken away from his handler and smashed in Kaysar's skull before fleeing the palace grounds. Some effort had been made to hunt down the creature, but it had vanished without a trace.

The boat jerked to a stop. Nnenia cut the tether lines of her web, wadded it up and ate it, not out of any consideration for the servants but because she might need the silk later.

Subira had wanted her to make the trip in human form, but Nnenia had refused. She had never felt comfortable in her human body, even before her destiny as the Spider Queen had been revealed. Besides, she argued, Subira's servants would have enough to do without having to care for a seasick old woman as well.

The Falcon King had carried them down from the volcano to the town where Subira had arranged to supervise the purchase of goods for the royal household. Nnenia had agreed to Subira's request that she not go wandering around the barge and remain out of sight. The protective magic of the First Ones did not extend to human activity and Nnenia could be squashed just as dead as any other spider.

She heard Subira send her handmaidens ahead to see if the palanquin was ready. She then reached under the bed and Nnenia crawled into her hand and up her arm to her shoulder hiding under the folds of the red cape Subira wore.

As Subira disembarked from the barge, Nnenia was bombarded by noise and smells. Human voices blended together in such confusion that she was amazed they could understand each other at all. Mixed in was the creaking of wheels, the groaning of slaves, the cracking of whips and the various grunts and snorts from beasts of burden.

The waste from those same beasts mingled with the body odors of the humans, and the somewhat salty smell of the lake itself. She could also catch whiffs of fragrant woods, bananas, coconuts, coffee beans, spices, meats and fishes. Nnenia buried her head into the perfumed folds of Subira's cape. The lilac fragrance wasn't as potent in the open air, but at least it was enough to smother the stench of the docks.

Thankfully, their route to the palace did not pass through the city. The late Banu-shah had persuaded her husband to have a private road built. She'd claimed it caused less disruption. Nnenia didn't much care about that, but she was thankful to be spared the chaos of the city. The docks had been bad enough.

As wife of the Grand Vizier, Subira lived with her husband in his chambers. The harem was reserved for the women of the Bade-shah's household: his wives and concubines, his maiden sisters and daughters, as well as any unmarried close female relatives under his protection.

When they arrived Subira's husband was sharing coffee with the Bade-shah's sons-in-law. Nnenia had tasted all of them and she had no qualms about any of them taking the throne. They all had their flaws to be sure. Rashad, a former warrior-slave, could barely write his own name. Zohan, a brilliant poet, seldom paid attention to what was going on around him. But these, and the flaws of their brothers-in-law, could be managed or tolerated. In Nnenia's opinion Suled was the worst. His fear of drowning was such that he refused to bathe in water, but rather coated his body in perfume. She noticed he had been given the seat nearest the open window. In the event he was not named the heir, he would almost certainly be appointed Lord of the Treasury since he had mastered the intricacies of trade that Nnenia did not care to understand.

She had judged them all and found them satisfactory. The Council had agreed. They did not demand perfection for they knew that to be impossible with humans. After all, a king with a cracked singing voice who nonetheless insisted on performing at state banquets was by far more preferable to one who taxed his people into poverty to sate his own gluttony.

Subira exchanged civilities with each of her husband's guests. When she spoke to Suled, Nnenia took the opportunity to climb down to the window ledge and out to the exterior wall of the palace.

It took her a few moments to orient herself. Subira had provided a map to the prince's apartments. Even from this height she could hear the frantic bustle in the courtyard as all guests for tonight's banquet arrived. She wasn't too worried though. She preferred to taste her subjects as they slept anyway. Once she arrived in the correct chamber she found a comfortable nook and settled in to wait.

The moon had climbed out of view before the prince staggered in clearly drunk. He just barely remembered to remove his sandals before collapsing onto the bed. Nnenia would have preferred he be sober, but perhaps it was better this way. With his senses dulled by wine and beer he was unlikely to notice her. She crept across the silk sheets, found a promising vein and bit.

The bitterness nearly made her retch. It was an unholy mix of spoiled meat, rotted yams, and curdled milk. And under all of it was the undeniable grittiness of a heart that delighted in cruelty.

Nnenia let her venom flow. Generally, she took no pleasure in killing, but as she made her way back out the window, she felt a kind of satisfaction in having done her duty.

Vengeance

By Peter J. Borger

It was a foggy morning, but I knew the sun would burn it off by nine or ten, it had already lifted to the trees as I walked over to get my boat from the end of Jerry's dock at about eight. Mornings on the lake have always been a favorite with me, the fog always makes you feel like you're in a land of make believe.

As I walked out on Jerry's dock I came to screeching halt. A giant water spider was sunning itself on the end of the pier right in my path. This was the biggest spider I have ever seen, about four or five inches in diameter, and the body was at least two inches wide. Not to be stopped, I picked up an oar from one of the boats in the slip and raised it. "Enough for you," I said aloud and brought the oar down on the thing. I hit it square in the body with the edge of the oar expecting a splat, but when I lifted the oar, it was still in one piece and seemed to shake off the hit. It began to run toward me and I dropped the oar and ran back to my cabin. I felt a little silly running from a spider, but the thing really scared me as it came at me with malice.

We had always fished in northern Wisconsin at the little set of cabins on Spider Lake, but I had never seen a spider that big before, even here. My cabin was smaller and around an outcropping in the lake with its own dock, and I had been at Jerry's cabin with the others the night before. We'd had a few beers and played some poker after a day's fishing on the lake. I was a bit buzzed when I left, and Jerry and Tom had told me to leave my boat at the dock and walk to my cabin to avoid any hassles from the DNR people, but I hadn't counted on that spider in the morning.

After a cup of coffee, I walked back to the dock and looked around. No spider was evident so I got in my boat and rowed myself around the outcropping toward my dock. While I was rowing, the spider crawled up on the front of the boat from the side and jumped to the front seat. I was completely freaked, never ever seeing a spider jump like that before and it terrified me as I didn't know if this one was venomous. I dived into the water and looked back. The spider crawled up on the edge of the boat and jumped into the water. I swam like hell for shore, leaving my boat adrift, but soaking my wallet and my cell phone. Thank God for waterproof phones. I dragged myself up on shore and went to the cabin to dry off. I called Jerry, and told him my boat had come loose from his dock and drifted by my cabin. He told me he'd take the motor boat and fetch it as soon as he dressed. I didn't want them knowing what a coward I was with my fear of spiders.

Feeling a little foolish, I made some breakfast and got some dry clothes on. Later, Jerry and Tom picked me up in the motor boat for more fishing, and we went out. I didn't tell them about the incident with the spider, feeling I'd be a laughingstock for the last day of the trip. We had a good day of fishing, and I left the incident behind me. We filleted our fish and fried them at Jerry's cabin, and were ready to pack up and leave in the morning.

When I got back to my cabin, I packed up my things in preparation to leave, but the spider haunted my dreams and I woke in a cold sweat. The moon was full and as I looked up through the window, the spider was outside on the window pane. When I turned on the light and looked again, it was gone, but as much as I tried, I couldn't go back to sleep. I made some coffee and cleaned up the kitchen goods, putting the coffee in my travel cup. I grabbed my grip and opened the door to go. The spider was on the stoop and walking toward me. I slammed the door and headed for the back door, slipped out, got in my car and headed for Highway Fifty-one, relieved to be away from the spider and Spider Lake.

I was past Wausau on my way down to Madison when the spider crawled up on the hood of my car. Crawling toward my windshield, I decided to go fast enough to blow the bugger off the car so I sped up to eighty, eighty-five. Here he was straining to stay on. Ninety, he was still crawling up my windshield and went out of sight on top. There were police lights behind me, and I knew I was in trouble. I stopped and the officer, though very business-like, bawled me out for going twenty-five miles over the speed limit. I took the ticket, but looking at the back window, found it was open. Not by much, but it worried me more than the ticket. I stopped at the next rest area and searched the car thoroughly. No spider. Relieved, I continued down Fifty-one.

Just coming to Lake DuBay, the spider crawled out of the defrosting vent in the front of the car and stood on the dashboard. I hit the brakes and knew he was about to jump, threw up my arms to protect my face. The car careened off the highway, rolled, and crashed into a pier on Lake DuBay. I could feel the water coming in but I was more terrified of the spider. I looked everywhere as the car began to sink. As I searched for the spider, I saw a splintered oar sticking out of my chest and knew I was in a bad way. As I struggled to unhook my seat belt, I saw the spider sitting on the oar. I tried to get out, but the oar had me pinned to the seat so I figured I'd had it. I reached for the spider figuring the least I could do was take it with me, but it backed up and just looked at me. The damned spider just looked at me and he looked odd to me. As the water overtook the car he just calmly swam to the surface. It was then I realized why he looked odd.

The damned thing was smiling.

Afterword

Peter J. Borger, was born on March 20, 1947 in Elmhurst, IL, where he was raised. He graduated from Immaculate Conception High School, Elmhurst College (BA), National Louis University (MA), and Northern Illinois University (PhD).

During his threescore and ten he taught math and worked a computer programmer. He wrote novels, and short-stories. He was a member of St. Petronille's church, a frequent swimmer at the Glen Ellyn YMCA, and a regular coffee-drinker at the Denny's on Schmale Road.

A long-time resident of Glen Ellyn, IL, he passed away November 28, 2017. He left behind children and grandchildren, his brothers and sister, many nieces and nephews, and friends.

An avid animal lover, perhaps it is no surprise that, in Pete's story, the spider triumphed over the human.